THE MOST FABULOUS STORY EVER TOLD

AND

Mr. Charles, Currently of Palm Beach

THE MOST FABULOUS STORY EVER TOLD

AND

Mr. Charles, Currently of Palm Beach

Two plays by

Paul Rudnick

THE OVERLOOK PRESS
Woodstock & New York

First published in the United States in 2000 by
The Overlook Press, Peter Mayer Publishers, Inc.
Lewis Hollow Road
Woodstock, New York 12498
www.overlookpress.com

Library of Congress Cataloging-in-Publication Data

Rudnick, Paul.
[Most fabulous story ever told ; and, Mr. Charles,
currently of Palm Beach / Paul Rudnick.
p. cm.
1. Bible—History of Biblical events—Drama. 2. Palm Beach (Fla.)—Drama.
3. Gays—Drama. I. Title: Most fabulous story ever told ; and, Mr. Charles,
currently of Palm Beach. II. Rudnick, Paul. Mr. Charles, currently of Palm
Beach. III. Title: Mr. Charles, currently of Palm Beach. IV. Title
PS3568.U334 M67 2000 812'.54—dc21 00-026617

Book design and type formatting by Bernard Schleifer
Manufactured in the United States of America
FIRST EDITION
1 3 5 7 9 8 6 4 2
ISBN 1-58567-052-9 (pk) ISBN 1058567-102-9 (hc)

For John Raftis

INTRODUCTION

The Most Fabulous Story Ever Told was sparked by the fundamentalist remark "God made Adam and Eve, not Adam and Steve"; this is about as blithe as fundamentalists tend to get. Sometime around 1996, a thought occurred to me—well, what if God had started things off with two guys, and the first lesbians as well, Jane and Mabel? Certainly my version of Biblical matters could be every bit as absurd as the King James take. Creation tales tend toward the delirious; trying to explain the cosmos inevitably leads to comedy. I quickly realized that mere Bible satire was not particularly satisfying and would grow wearisome for a full-length play; what I wanted to do was explore larger matters of faith through a frame of Biblical events.

Prior to *Most Fabulous*, I had written several plays that dealt with sex, now, in a post-Monica era, the least taboo of all preoccupations. Religion and the possible existence of God seemed like a much more provocative topic; friends are more than thrilled to offer Polaroids of their mating habits, but the question "Do you believe in God?" is far more personal. I didn't want to merely bash organized religion, although I was sorely tempted. It's almost impossible to find an atrocity unjustified by someone's belief in a higher power: Various capricious gods have commanded their flocks to start world wars, mutilate nonbelievers, and contribute their paychecks to cable-channel evangelists. I wanted to, however comically, research the roots of faith: Why do we need to believe? What terror or transcendence leads to either the invention or the discovery of a god? In humanity's earliest hours, the world was undoubtedly a horrifying locale: volcanoes, floods, and a lack of indoor plumbing and shampoo would naturally inspire a quest for larger reassurances, for the security of a divine plan. Act I of *Most Fabulous* follows two couples' adventures in creating civilization.These four individuals reach very different conclusions about the nature of nature. Act One is written in broad strokes, befitting the tumult of society's beginnings, and the characters don't age as they hurtle from the Garden to slavery in Egypt and beyond. Their motives, however, are not farcical but absolutely sincere. It was exhilarating to write about characters experiencing the most primal hurdles and joys, including the first sunrise and, literally, the first date.

Early on, I decided that two acts of Biblical revisionism were unnecessary; the Old Testament was plenty. In Act II I wanted to trace the modern-day results of Act I, to see where faith has landed in contemporary Manhattan. The personalities, opinions, and lusts of our four main characters remain intact, only the quartet have no memory of their lives before the intermission. Adam is now a teacher at a ritzy private school, Steve is a contractor, and Jane and Mabel are awaiting the birth of a child. The trick in all this was to make *Most Fabulous* feel like a single play, and not two vaguely related one-acts. I was particularly inspired by the nimble time-travel of works like Caryl Churchill's delicious *Cloud Nine* and the gleeful, yet passionate theatricality of Charles Ludlam. Primal innocence is no longer possible in Act Two, as the characters and the planet itself have seen too much; history has occurred. Still, a basic impulse toward the Almighty remains, whether the characters are coping with fetid arks, fretting Pharaohs, or the obscenity of AIDS.

I wrote *Most Fabulous* over a period of three years, and it was first staged in workshop form at the Williamstown Theatre Festival and then in full production at the New York Theatre Workshop, all in 1999. Both productions were gorgeously directed by Christopher Ashley, who was an essential guide in the play's incubation; I rewrite endlessly, and Christopher is the most patient, dedicated, and gifted cohort imaginable. Our aim was always to ground the play in both the highest and sometimes the most extreme comedy, and in an equally absolute reality. The stakes had to remain very true and enormous; however lunatic, the characters' lives had to matter. The mission was to create a style that could accommodate the dizzying leaps of Act One and the Christmas Eve immediacy of Act Two.

Audience and critical response to this play has been fascinating: I've learned that people are very touchy about God. Atheists demand a complete denial of any Biblical truth, and more religious types get very twitchy about, say, just what happened in that manger. Perhaps the most stolid and painful of all are the politically correct, who tremble over the most acceptable and positive portrayal of gay characters, and the most earnestly multicultural treatment of human history. I wanted to offend or provoke everyone equally, to allow all points of view equal mockery and equal acceptance. I didn't want the play to answer impossible questions. Some audience members bizarrely looked to the play as they would to any religious text: They wanted inarguable proof, a complete and tidy explanation of humankind, without irreverence.

For me, the play's pivotal moment comes toward the end of Act II, when Adam's deeply held belief in a loving God and a just universe is truly shaken, when he faces, for the first time in the play, a life without Steve. Until this moment, death has never really entered the equation; suddenly, Adam is overwhelmed by the unknowable. Steve offers Adam a much-coveted cashmere sweater and asks, "Do you feel better now? About my dying, and losing your faith?" Adam, confronting the largest possible questions, can only look at Steve, stroke the cashmere, and acknowledge the true, inescapable insanity of life by replying, "Yes!" This scene, I hope, expresses the impossibility of ultimate knowledge, the baffling, inherent tragedy of love and death, and the divine wonder that is triple-ply cashmere. I realize that such philosophical grandeur is an awful lot to ask of one Christmas present, but then again, it's a really nice sweater. One critic was particularly outraged by this moment and felt that I was depicting the triumph of luxury goods over compassion. Some people just don't get it, or maybe that petulant critic had only worn shetland.

Most Fabulous was protested, primarily by a single group fanatically dedicated to enshrining the reputation of Mary. No one from this sect ever saw or read the play, or seemed to realize that Mary wasn't a character in the work; they instead chose, in a dimwitted crusade, to inundate the theater with identical postcards and the occasional scrawled letter. Most of their thoughts were along the lines of "Mary is a symbol of all-knowing grace and infinite love, and She forgives you for writing this play, you disgusting Kike cocksucker!" My favorite of these missives, often written on soothing pastel stationery, concluded with the phrase "Would appreciate a reply." My only wish is that such misguided penpals at some point actually see the play, or any play for that matter; the ignorance and chirpy bile of such fundamentalist hate-mail is a handy example of faith gone dangerously astray. And why would anyone want to believe in a God without a sense of humor?

Another response to *Most Fabulous* involved the question of stereotypes: Some audience members worried about the play's depiction of less-than-macho gay males and delightfully butch lesbians. This attitude is the PC version of good-Christian zeal; self-righteous liberals prefer only idealized, wholesome, and ultimately lifeless portrayals of perfected gay role models. Adam, for example, enjoys hair care and laundry; he is also the most consumingly curious, adventurous and romantic character onstage. Jane is proudly bullish, and also wry, loving, and fearless. Where's the stereotype? Butch lesbians especially tend to make the quiveringly correct very anxious; I prefer to celebrate the two-fisted glory of Jane. Gay lives are as infinitely varied as those of straight folks, but why banish extremely realistic behavior simply because it doesn't suit the tolerance brochure? Besides, for most petty-minded lifestyle watchdogs, becoming a stereotype would be a step up.

My other goal in writing *Most Fabulous* was to intertwine two near-epic love stories with my particular retelling of Bible lore. I wanted the pairings of Adam and Steve and Jane and Mabel to be buffeted and tested by their voyage from Eden to Chelsea; they find that God and love can be redundant, or a contradiction in terms. I hope that audiences will care deeply about the fates of these characters and their couplings. I worship the god of romantic comedy. Writing *Most Fabulous* was an enormous challenge, in terms of everything from structure to the banality of dealing with the Big Questions. I haven't resolved any of these difficulties, but that's why I wrote the play: to push myself as a writer, to see what I thought about such devastatingly embarrassing issues as God and Chanukah, and to try to surprise and entertain an audience primed for controversy.

Staging *Most Fabulous* is what I like to think of as a directorial Everest: The first act alone requires the creation of the world, the first brunch, and a sexually predatory pig. At Williamstown, Chris Ashley and our amazing scenic designer, Mike Brown, solved the play's daunting design obstacles on a shoe-box-sized stage, using painted panels, an army of stagehands, and far more ingenuity than cash. At the New York Theatre Workshop, Mike and Chris created a physically stunning world, centered on a full-stage, faded Renaissance fresco that split open, revealing everything from a blue-silk flood to an Egyptian/Vegas backdrop of glittering Keith Haring-inspired hieroglyphs. Both productions were graced by extraordinary casts of actors capable of the most ardent emotion and the most outrageous comedy. Speed was essential; comedy is always best when played for pace and for keeps. If *Most Fabulous* is only acted as a romp, or a jokebook, it will quickly become tiresome; the characters must wholeheartedly believe in the violence and exaltation of their many situations. The Egyptian guards' spears may be cardboard, but the threat to Mabel and Steve's lives must be very real. Alan Tudyk played Adam in both productions, with a superb blend of innocence, irresistible humor, and yearning, and he made it all look effortless—he was very much the soul of the play. Becky Ann Baker created Jane in both productions, with a peerless mix of strength, common sense, and, in her birth monologue, hilarious fury. All of the roles listed for Actor #1, from a latecomer in the audience to the haughtiest of Boy-Kings to a majestically acid Santa, were written for Peter Bartlett, an actor whose genius is a Christmas gift to any playwright. I treasure all of our cast members, for taking every possible risk and for believing, if not in God, then in the possibilities of theater. I would like to expecially mention two wonderful actresses who displalyed particular valor in playing the role of Mabel in New York: Jenny Bacon, who broke her foot onstage, and somehow continued her pagan dance, and Kathryn Meisle, who took over the role on about ten seconds notice, a very few days before we opened. I would also like to thank both Williamstown and the New York Theatre Workshop, for their overwhelming support of this play, and a most fabulous team of producers who moved the play for a commercial run.

When I wrote *Most Fabulous*, I knew that people would ask me if I believed in God. The play is my answer, but that's a little easy. I think I believe in the transcendence of art, in that perishable moment when an audience and a performer and a play work together, when laughter and technique and emotion create a conspiracy of pleasure. I believe in theater and style and Chris Ashley; I believe in what human beings can do when you give them fifty bucks to buy some cheap red polyester velvet. Some people need more, something with vengeance and commandments and jihads. All I need to keep going, to stay spiritual, is Peter Bartlett in a Santa suit.

— Paul Rudnick

THE MOST FABULOUS STORY EVER TOLD

AND

Mr. Charles, Currently of Palm Beach

THE MOST FABULOUS STORY EVER TOLD was originally produced by the Williamstown Theatre Festival (Michael Ritchie, Producer), in Williamstown, Massachusetts, on July 1, 1998. It was directed by Christopher Ashley; the set design was by Michael Brown; the costume design was by Marion Williams; the lighting design was by Rui Rita; the sound design was by Kurt B. Kellenberger; and the stage manager was Judith Tucker. The cast was as follows:

STAGE MANAGER . . . . Dara Fisher
ADAM . . . . Alan Tudyk
STEVE . . . . Bobby Cannavale
MATINEE LADY, WHISKERS,
MOM #1, FTATATEETA,
RABBI SHARON KLOPER . . . . Maggie Moore
PRIEST, BUGS, RHINO, DAD #2, BRAD,
KEVIN MARKHAM . . . . Michael Wiggins
LATECOMER, PETER, ZIZI, DAD #1,
PHARAOH, TREY POMFRET . . . . Peter Bartlett
CHERYL MINDLE, MITTENS, FIFI,
MOM #2, PEGGY . . . . .Michi Barall
JANE . . . . Becky Ann Baker
MABEL . . . . Jessica Hecht

THE MOST FABULOUS STORY EVER TOLD was originally produced by New York Theatre Workshop, in New York City, on December 14, 1998, and subsequently produced off-Broadway by Scott Rudin, Viertel/Frankel/Baruch/Routh, Paramount Pictures, Maxwell/Balsam/Harris, and the New York Theatre Workshop, at the Minetta Lane Theatre, on February 2, 1999. It was directed by Christopher Ashley; the set design was by Michael Brown; the costume design was by Susan Hilferty; the lighting design was by Donald Holder; the sound design was by Darron L. West; and the production stage manager was Charles Means. The cast was as follows:

STAGE MANAGER . . . . Amy Sedaris
ADAM . . . . Alan Tudyk
STEVE . . . . Juan Carlos Hernandez
FATHER JOSEPH, BUGS, RHINO,
DAD #2, BRAD, KEVIN MARKHAM . . . .Orlando Pabotoy
MIRIAM MILLER, BABE, MOM #1,
FTATATEETA, RABBI SHARON . . . . Lisa Kron
LATECOMER, PETER, DAD #1,
PHARAOH, TREY POMFRET . . . . Peter Bartlett
CHERYL MINDLE, FLUFFY, MOM #2,
PEGGY . . . . Joanna P. Adler
JANE . . . . Becky Ann Baker
MABEL . . . . Kathryn Meisle

At the Minetta Lane Theatre the role of STAGE MANAGER was performed by Peg Healey, and the role of STEVE was performed by Jay Goede.

ACT I

Throughout the play, the audience will hear the STAGE MANAGER*'s voice, amplified through a microphone, calling various cues for sound, lights, and scenery. The play begins with the curtain down.*

STAGE MANAGER'S VOICE

House to half, go, house out and pre-set, go. Creation of the world, go.

The curtain rises on a bare stage, in darkness. The STAGE MANAGER *sits at a small table or desk, at the side of the stage. She is a sleek, incredibly capable woman, dressed in a black turtleneck and close-fitting pants. She wears her microphone on a headset, leaving her hands free. She speaks in a low, authoritative, sexy voice, like a very smart flight attendant with an agenda. She is the ultimate professional: confident, aloof, and slightly swaggering. She knows what she's doing.*

Music begins, something grand and propulsive, like Wagnerian pop or a rolling, percolating dance mix of "Thus Sprach Zarathustra."

STAGE MANAGER

Monday, go. Light, go. I love this.

A shaft of light hits the stage. More light appears, illuminating the bare stage from every possible direction. Finally, the entire stage is ablaze with blinding white light.

STAGE MANAGER

First sunset, go.

The stage returns to darkness.

STAGE MANAGER

Tuesday, go. Oceans, go.

The stage is again filled with light. Yards of blue silk are released from high above the stage, cascading to the stage floor, shimmering and undulating. Sounds of the ocean are heard. The silk is then either mechanically removed, or the STAGE MANAGER *leaves her desk, gathers up the fabric, and stashes it in a corner. All of this happens very quickly, as the music builds.*

STAGE MANAGER

Sunset at the beach, go.

The light is again extinguished.

STAGE MANAGER

Wednesday, go. Land, go.

The lights come up. A large rock, suitable for sitting on, is now tugged center stage, either mechanically or by the STAGE MANAGER, *using a rope. A horizon line appears in the distance.*

STAGE MANAGER

Sunset over the mountains, go.

Blackness.

STAGE MANAGER

Thursday, go. Garden of Eden, go.

The lights come up, as the Garden of Eden begins to fill the stage.

STAGE MANAGER

Sunset in paradise, go.

Blackness.

STAGE MANAGER

Friday, go. Creatures of the earth, go.

Lights up on the full garden. We now hear sounds of animal life, everything from barking dogs to laughing monkeys to roaring lions. The sounds should be vigorous but happy. The STAGE MANAGER *slaps a mosquito which has landed on her neck. She squashes a bug with her foot.*

STAGE MANAGER

Sunset at the zoo, go.

Blackness.

STAGE MANAGER

Saturday, noon-ish, go.

The lights come up on the Garden, gorgeously sunlit, as we hear something like the "I had a dream" notes from "Everything's Coming Up Roses" in the musical Gypsy.

ADAM *enters, perhaps through a door upstage center. He is an attractive, innocent, wide-eyed fellow in his twenties. He wears only a jockstrap. He looks around, filled with a combination of wonder, awe, and shock. Throughout the play,* ADAM *will remain overwhelmingly, passionately curious, in love with the world's possibilities. His ebullient, aggressive need to know everything will always hurtle him joyously forward.*

ADAM

(after a beat)

Hello?

(a beat)

Yes?

(looking around)

Well. *My.*

(He looks around, really taking in the garden, more and more impressed)

Whoa. Nice! Very nice! And there are trees and flowers, and a clear blue sky . . .

(ADAM has now leapt atop the rock, and he studies the landscape)

I mean, I would put the lake over *there,* but—I am so jazzed about this! All right, I'll just say it, right out loud—this garden is fabulous! Stop it!

Wait. Who am I talking to? Where am I? Who am I? What am I? Am I—gay?

(He thinks for a second, and then, with exuberant, grateful relief)

Yes!

(He carefully checks his hair, smoothing the sides into place)

And I'm alone.

The STAGE MANAGER strikes a crisp, bell-like note on a small chime. STEVE enters, from the wings, or any different entrance than ADAM's. STEVE is a handsome guy, a bit more solid than ADAM. He is good-natured but firm in his opinions, and more grounded than ADAM. He also wears only a jock-strap. He and ADAM spot each other with huge enthusiasm.

STEVE

Hey!

ADAM

Hey!

STEVE

Hey!

ADAM

Hey!

(awkwardly extending his hand, inventing the hand-shake)

Adam.

STEVE

Steve.

(they shake hands vigorously)

ADAM

Nice to meet you!

STEVE

Yeah!

ADAM

Really nice!

STEVE

(perhaps taking an appreciative glance at ADAM*'s body)*

Yeah.

ADAM

Can I ask you something?

STEVE

Sure!

ADAM

(with great urgency, the words tumbling out, all in one breath)

Where did we come from? How did we get here? Who made us, who made this garden, and why? Are we the only ones here, are we meant to be together, are there things we're supposed to do, how will we know, will our relationship be good for the both of us, will we be together forever, what's forever, and is all of this part of some plan, or did it just happen?

STEVE

(a bit overwhelmed)

I should go.

ADAM

Oh, oh, me too.

STEVE

Good to meet you.

ADAM

Can I . . . can I see you again?

STEVE

I'd like that.

ADAM

But how will I find you?

STEVE

Call me.

ADAM

(After a beat, yelling)

Steve!

STEVE

Yeah?

STAGE MANAGER

First date, go.

ADAM and STEVE begin walking together, through the garden, appreciating their surroundings. They share the giddy nervousness of a first date.

ADAM

(pointing)

Grass!

STEVE

(pointing)

Vine!

ADAM

(pointing)

Rock!

STEVE sits on the rock, gesturing for ADAM to join him. ADAM sits beside him, and STEVE rapidly puts his arm around ADAM's shoulders.

STEVE

First base.

ADAM

(pointing to STEVE's feet)

Feet!

STEVE

(pointing to ADAM's knees)

Knees!

ADAM

(pointing to STEVE's stomach)

Abs!

STEVE

(pointing to ADAM's arms)

Arms!

ADAM

(pointing to STEVE's hands)

Fingernails!

STEVE

(looking into ADAM's eyes)

Eyes.

ADAM

(pointing to STEVE's lips)

Soft face-hole things.

STEVE *leans over to kiss* ADAM. ADAM *pulls away, confused.*

What . . . what are you doing?

STEVE

I . . . I don't know. I just—I wanted to put my soft face-hole things on yours.

ADAM

Really? Why?

STEVE

I don't know. I just, I was looking at your soft face-hole things, and I just—if you don't want to, it's okay . . .

ADAM

No, no, I mean, it's just . . .

ADAM *turns his head away for a second, and cups his hand over his mouth, exhaling sharply and checking his breath. Satisfied, he turns back to* STEVE.

Sure!

ADAM *and* STEVE *kiss. The kiss begins extremely awkwardly, as they aim their open mouths at each other, but end up landing on chins or cheeks. Gradually, slurping and contorting, they achieve a real kiss.* ADAM *then pulls away, and runs a few yards away.*

STEVE

I'm sorry!

ADAM

No, no, don't be . . .

STEVE

What's wrong?

ADAM

It's just, when I first got here, I thought that everything was perfect. And now it just got—more perfect!

ADAM *runs back to* STEVE, *and they kiss again, even more passionately. Things begin getting a bit physical.*

STAGE MANAGER

Boners, go.

ADAM *runs away again, even more hyper and upset.*

ADAM

Oh my!

STEVE

What?

ADAM

I just, I started to feel . . .

(He is getting an erection, to an almost painful degree. He begins to rub his crotch, to relieve the pressure.)

I'm sorry.

STEVE

No, don't be.

ADAM

But . . .

STEVE

(also rubbing his crotch)

I feel like that too!

ADAM

(panicking wildly)

What is happening to us?

STEVE

I have an idea.

ADAM

Yeah?

STEVE

What if I took my mouth, and my lips, and my tongue, but not my teeth, and I put them on your . . .

(indicating ADAM*'s crotch)*

ADAM

(thrilled)

You!

STEVE

(also delighted)

And later, you could do the same thing for me!

ADAM

(even more giddy)

Yes! If I wasn't too tired!

STEVE

Deal!

As STEVE *begins to kneel before Adam, we hear:*

STAGE MANAGER

Privacy, go.

The stage is plunged into blackness.

STAGE MANAGER'S VOICE

Sorry, folks. Oh, get over it!

From the darkness, we hear:

ADAM

Great idea! Thank you!

STEVE

(His mouth full, a bit garbled)

You're welcome!

(a beat, and then, not garbled)

I have another idea!

ADAM

(from the darkness)

OUCH!

STAGE MANAGER

Lights twenty-nine, go.

The lights come up. ADAM *is bent over the rock, facing the audience.* STEVE *stands close behind him; they're having anal sex. They both still wear their jockstraps. They will continue to have vigorous sex during the following conversation.*

STEVE

What, what's wrong?

ADAM

That hurts!

STEVE

I'm sorry—should I stop?

ADAM

No. It's just that I've never done this before, you know, using a person.

STEVE

What did you use?

ADAM

Well, those shiny green things, you know, that grow on the ground . . .

STEVE

Sure . . .

ADAM

Oh, and sometimes those pointy orange things, that grow under the ground . . .

STEVE

(interrupting)

Adam?

ADAM

Yes?

STEVE

Do you wish that I was, you know, more like those other things?

ADAM

No, oh no! You are wonderful, you are so special!

(continuing to have sex, ADAM *reaches around to slap* STEVE *on the thigh, encouragingly.)*

They were just . . .

STEVE

What?

ADAM

Salad!

STEVE *is relieved; the sex grows even more vigorous, as both guys begin moaning ecstatically with pleasure.*

STAGE MANAGER

Lights thirty, go.

The lights go out, as the sex continues.

STAGE MANAGER

First simultaneous orgasm ever, go.

From the darkness, we hear both men enjoy an exuberantly loud, enormously lusty and joyful orgasm.

STAGE MANAGER

Thank you, thank you. Lights thirty-one, go.

When the lights come up, the two men are seated back-to-back on the rock, their heads thrown back in post-orgasm afterglow. We hear sultry, sexy, film noir-ish saxophone music play. ADAM *is eating a banana, while* STEVE *munches a carrot, as if they were both smoking post-coital cigarettes.*

STEVE

Adam?

ADAM

Right here.

STEVE

I love you.

ADAM

What?

STEVE

I love you.

ADAM

What's that?

STEVE

Love is—well, it's hard to explain it, exactly.

ADAM

Is it that thing that makes you bring me presents?

STEVE

(handing ADAM *a small rock)*
Here's another rock.

ADAM

(thrilled)
Thank you!
*(*ADAM *extends his arm and places the rock on his ring finger, considering the rock as if it were a diamond engagement ring; he's very pleased)*

STEVE

Love is—something I know. I don't know how we got here, I don't know why touching you makes me so happy, but I know—that seeing you, or even thinking about seeing you, makes me feel like—I don't need to know anything else.

ADAM

Really?

STEVE

You're my answer.

ADAM *stands and strides away from* STEVE, *across the stage.*

STEVE

What? What is it?

ADAM

I just . . . you didn't kiss me, and I didn't fall down, but—I can't catch my breath. It's that thing, that you said.

STEVE

I love you?

ADAM

Stop! Don't! I can't—I can't look at you.

STEVE

Why not?

ADAM

Because I will break, I will burst, into one million tiny pieces of joy! I will be so happy that I won't be able to be a creature anymore, I'll become—pure happiness!

STEVE *has begun to pursue* ADAM *all over the stage.* ADAM *might end up standing on the rock, across the stage from* STEVE.

STEVE

You will?

ADAM

So I have to stay just like this, perfectly still, frozen, so I can always be someone who just heard you say, "I love you."

STEVE

Adam?

ADAM

(not looking at him)
I can't.

STEVE

(enjoying the chase)
This is really fun. I can torture you.

ADAM

Stay away!

STEVE

Here I come . . .

ADAM

Stop! I'm not looking!

STEVE

I love you! I love you!

ADAM

No! No more!

STEVE

Okay. Good-bye.

STEVE *begins to stride offstage, away from* ADAM.

ADAM

What? Steve?

STEVE

(pausing)
Yeah?

ADAM

(after a beat)

I love you.

They run to each other, and begin to make love. The sultry saxophone music is heard again. ADAM *and* STEVE *are now on the ground, kissing and embracing.*

FATHER JOSEPH

Stop!

ADAM

What?

FATHER JOSEPH

Stop it this minute!

ADAM

Excuse me?

FATHER JOSEPH MARKHAM, *a priest in traditional clerical garb, has stood up from a seat in the audience. He holds a small, leather-bound Bible. He is extremely angry; he just couldn't put up with* ADAM *and* STEVE*'s story for one more second.*

Only ADAM *will interact with the audience members. Once* ADAM *is standing,* STEVE *will remain on the ground, asleep.*

FATHER JOSEPH

I'm Father Joseph Markham, and I'm sorry, but this is all wrong! It wasn't Adam and Steve, that's nonsense! This isn't the Bible!

ADAM

The Bible? What's the Bible?

MIRIAM

Don't ask!

MIRIAM MILLER, *a matinee lady, has stood up from her seat in the front row. She wears a nice dress from Loehmann's, accessorized with gold jewelry, an important purse and maybe a coordinated shawl. She is not shy. She introduces herself, in a friendly manner, to* ADAM *and the audience.*

MIRIAM

I'm Miriam Miller, and I'm with the theater party from Temple Beth El. And I like this story! I think it's very sweet!

STAGE MANAGER

Houselights!

LATECOMER

Oh, I'm sorry!

As the houselights come up, illuminating the entire audience, a LATE-

COMER *has entered the theater, coming down an aisle from the back of the house. He is nattily dressed and carries several shopping bags from upscale stores. He is a sophisticated, highly strung Manhattanite.*

ADAM

Who are you? All of you?

LATECOMER

I'm late, I'm sorry, but I had my mother and my shrink and my AA meeting, so I needed to shop.

MIRIAM

(sympathetically)

Of course.

ADAM

Shop?

LATECOMER

What have I missed?

MIRIAM

Well, the world got created.

FATHER JOSEPH

The wrong world!

MIRIAM

But it's gorgeous, like Aruba, or Cancun.

ADAM

Cancun? What's Cancun?

LATECOMER

It's over.

MIRIAM

And then these two guys showed up.

LATECOMER

Two guys?

ADAM

Steve and me!

FATHER JOSEPH

Which is not historically accurate! I have pamphlets!

(He offers pamphlets to real audience members)

Do you want some pamphlets?

ADAM

(excited and curious)

Wait! Everybody! Where are you all from? Is there a world—outside the garden?

FATHER JOSEPH

Of course!

MIRIAM

No, no! Oh no!

LATECOMER

Take a look!

ADAM

How?

LATECOMER

Climb a tree!

ADAM *runs to a tree, or the proscenium, and begins climbing, as high as he can get.*

MIRIAM

Stop! It's a wonderful garden! You have fruit, you have foliage, don't push it!

ADAM

(eagerly)

But why not? So far it's all been fabulous! Why can't I see everything?

LATECOMER

Why can't he see more?

MIRIAM

Because it's a terrible world! It's unpleasant! He'll find out things he doesn't want to know!

ADAM

Like what?

FATHER JOSEPH

(holding up his Bible)

It's all right in here!

LATECOMER

According to whom?

FATHER JOSEPH

According to the truth!

MIRIAM

According to you!

ADAM

But I want to know who made me! And why! I want to thank them, for everything! For Steve! I want . . .

FATHER JOSEPH

Revelation!

ADAM

Yes!

MIRIAM

(now standing near the front of the stage)

But shouldn't you ask your . . .

(She gestures at STEVE, *trying to find the correct term)*

friend, about leaving the garden?

ADAM

He loves me. I love him.

LATECOMER

(regarding STEVE*)*

He's heaven.

(to ADAM*)*

I hate you!

MIRIAM

But if you leave, things can happen. People can get hurt.

ADAM

(who's never heard the word before, and doesn't know what it means)

Hurt?

FATHER JOSEPH

They can betray the people they care about.

ADAM

Betray?

LATECOMER

You could lose—everything.

ADAM

But I don't understand! And I want to!

MIRIAM

You could be alone—again.

ADAM

No—Steve will come with me. We'll go together!

STAGE MANAGER

Adam, we need a decision.

ADAM

But what's out there? All I can see is more garden!

Adam, trying to see more, swings out from the tree and momentarily loses his footing. Everyone screams, as ADAM *regains his footing.*

STAGE MANAGER

(during the hubbub)

Heads up!

CHERYL

Adam?

CHERYL MINDLE, *a young woman from Utah, stands up in the audience. She is primly dressed and clutches her Playbill.*

ADAM

Yes?

CHERYL

I just got here, to the big city, from Utah. And I still don't have a place to live, or a steady job. And I'm really scared, and really excited. And Utah was great, but—I had to leave.

MIRIAM

But why?

LATECOMER

It was Utah.

CHERYL

To find out. What would happen. What comes next. If you don't take a chance, you'll never know anything!

STAGE MANAGER

Stand by, fifty-seven L and garden, out.

ADAM

Fifty-seven L?

STAGE MANAGER

(to ADAM*)*

Strike the garden? You have to call it.

MIRIAM

Don't!

FATHER JOSEPH

Learn!

LATECOMER

Why not?

CHERYL

Ask!

ADAM, *from his perch in the tree, looks at everyone. He takes a deep breath.*

ADAM

Show me . . .

(He looks at Steve)

Show us—everything!

STAGE MANAGER

And the cue?

ADAM

Fifty-seven L!

FATHER JOSEPH

Wait!

STAGE MANAGER

What?

FATHER JOSEPH

(going to the stage)

If you're going to leave the garden—take this.

(He places his Bible on the stage)

ADAM

Why?

FATHER JOSEPH

It is all you will ever really need.

MIRIAM

And take this too.

ADAM

What is it?

MIRIAM

(placing a small item from her purse atop the Bible)

A moist towelette.

STAGE MANAGER

Adam?

ADAM

Go!

There is a huge crash of sound and light, as the stage is plunged into darkness. A few seconds later, the lights come up on the stage. The garden has vanished. MIRIAM, FATHER JOSEPH, *the* LATECOMER, *and* CHERYL *are all gone. The stage is empty and harshly lit. The space is cavernous, dark, and frightening.*

ADAM *is now lying on the ground, having fallen from the tree.* STEVE *is gone.*

ADAM

(realizing he's been hurt in the fall)

Owww!

(looking around)

Steve? Steve?

(standing and searching for STEVE, *very frightened)*

Oh no! *Steve!*

STEVE *runs on. He and* ADAM *are now both truly naked.*

STEVE

What happened?

ADAM

(looking around)

Where . . . where did . . .

STEVE

(staring at ADAM*)*

Adam . . .

ADAM

Yeah?

STEVE

(stunned)

Adam—you're naked.

ADAM *looks down at his body; he is shocked and yelps, leaping about as if his body is suddenly a foreign object. He looks up at* STEVE.

ADAM

Steve . . .

STEVE

What?

ADAM

So are you!

*(*STEVE *looks down at his own body, shocked)*

You know what this means . . .

STEVE

I have to get to a gym!

ADAM

I need some khakis!

JANE *stalks onstage. She is a hefty, proudly and impressively butch woman, wearing a pair of primitive overalls made from leaves and bark.* JANE *is boisterous and tough-minded, with a short fuse. She is also very warm-hearted and generous, earthy and wonderfully sane. At the moment she is violently pissed off.*

JANE

What the hell are you doing?

ADAM *and* STEVE *both scream and try to cover their naked flesh.*

ADAM and STEVE

AHHH!

JANE

Oh, please! Like I could care!

ADAM

Who are you?

JANE

Jane.

MABEL

(from offstage)

Jane?

MABEL *runs onstage. She is a thin, quivering, sprite-like waif with a cloud of long, frizzy, pre-Raphaelite hair. She wears a long dress, also made from leaves and bark. She always responds emotionally to any situation; she is tremulous, hopeful, and sympathetic to everyone. As soon as* MABEL *sees* ADAM *and* STEVE, *she screams.*

AHHH!

ADAM and STEVE

(screaming right back)

AHHH!

MABEL

(regarding ADAM *and* STEVE*)*

Jane—who are those poor, ugly women?

JANE

They're not women. But I have a feeling they did something to the garden, and I'm gonna find out what!

MABEL

No, no—let me.

MABEL *approaches* ADAM *and* STEVE, *gingerly. She speaks in her best, hostess-y manner, using a loud, distinct voice, as if talking to children.*

MABEL

Hel-lo.

ADAM: Hi.
STEVE: Hello. } *(at the same time)*

MABEL

(pointing to JANE*)*

Jane.

(pointing to herself, perhaps with a curtsey)

And Mabel.

ADAM

What are you?

JANE

We're the first people!

ADAM

Excuse me?

MABEL

(graciously)

We're the first human beings ever. We were living in the garden, enjoying eternal peace and happiness.

ADAM

(condescending)

I'm sorry.

JANE

Yeah, what?

ADAM

I was actually the first person.

STEVE

(to ADAM*)*

You were not.

ADAM

Yes I was. I got there first.

STEVE

And what was I?

ADAM

The first boyfriend.

JANE

Excuse me, buddy!

STEVE

What?

JANE

We were here first. We were sitting in that garden, minding our own business . . .

MABEL

(sweetly)

Enjoying all the wonder of nature . . .

JANE

When somebody came along after us, and *fucked things up!*

STEVE

How do you know? Maybe you're the ones who fucked things up! Maybe the garden was getting a little crowded!

JANE

It was a women's garden!

MABEL

Although we had special nights for other creatures, with discussion groups . . .

STEVE

It was *our garden!*

JANE

You wanna make something of it?

STEVE

Try me!

STEVE *and* JANE *face off, circling each other, balling up their fists, preparing for a fight.*

ADAM

Steve, don't!

MABEL

Violence is never the answer—look at what happened to your breasts!

JANE

(taunting STEVE*)*

Come on, nature boy . . .

STEVE

(to JANE*)*

Hey, who cut your hair? Lightning?

As STEVE *turns toward* ADAM *to laugh at his wisecrack,* JANE *shoves* STEVE *from behind. He stumbles and turns on her.*

JANE

Hit me! Come on, pal! You want a piece of this?

STEVE

You're not a man! I bet you don't even have a dick!

MABEL

We have vaginas! They're our friends!

JANE

Faggot!

STEVE

Dyke!

Just as STEVE *and* JANE *lunge forward and are about to hit each other,* ADAM, *in agony, stops the bout.*

ADAM

Stop it! It's all my fault! I ruined the garden!

STEVE

You did?

JANE

I knew it!

ADAM

I climbed a tree, and I was asking questions, and then the garden disappeared!

JANE

(incredulous, pissed off)

You were asking questions?

STEVE

Why?

ADAM

And now Steve and I are naked!

MABEL

We were naked too!

ADAM

And what happened?

JANE

The minute the garden disappeared . . .

(referring to MABEL*)*

she got crazy. She started jogging.

MABEL

Do I look fat?

JANE

No!

STEVE

(to JANE*)*

And what did you do?

JANE

Nothing! I like my body.

ADAM

So why are you wearing clothes?

JANE

I need pockets.

STAGE MANAGER

North wind, go

We hear sounds of gusting wind, and the rumble of approaching thunder.

ADAM

(shivering)

It's windy.

STAGE MANAGER

Goosebumps, go.

For the first time in their lives, ADAM, STEVE, JANE, *and* MABEL *feel the effects of bad weather; they are starting to feel very lost and exposed.*

JANE

It's gonna rain.

MABEL

We have to get inside!

STEVE

Inside *what?*

MABEL

Where are we?

ADAM

The world.

STAGE MANAGER

Lightning, go. Thunder, go. Barren wilderness, go.

There is a huge clap of thunder and a bolt of lightning; the stage is plunged into darkness.

Campfire, go.

The lights come up on a small area of the stage. JANE *and* MABEL *are asleep together, on the ground.* STEVE *sits up, wrapped in a blanket, unable to sleep.* ADAM, *also in a blanket, sits nearby. The light from the campfire casts eerie shadows.*

ADAM

Steve?

(STEVE *refuses to speak to* ADAM*)*

Is everyone really mad at me? You know, just because the garden disappeared and we're in a barren wilderness and there's no food and we're starting to smell?

STEVE

Why didn't you ask me? About leaving the garden?

ADAM

Because I thought that you might—say no.

STEVE

Bingo!

ADAM

But—I've never heard you talk like this. You sound like I've—hurt you.

(For the first time, ADAM *realizes the meaning of the word "hurt")*

STEVE

You did!

ADAM

Hey. Hey, Mister Cranky-Face. Mister-I-got-kicked-out-of-Paradise-so-I'm-not-gonna-smile.

STEVE

That's right!

ADAM

(spotting an object a few yards away)

Oh come on—look! Everything didn't vanish! We still have—this!

ADAM *has run over to pick up the Bible, which* FATHER JOSEPH *had left on the stage. He brings the Bible back to* STEVE.

STEVE

What's that?

ADAM

(investigating the Bible; neither he nor STEVE *has any concept of books or reading)*

I'm not sure. It's filled with these little markings.

STEVE *rips a page out of the Bible and begins eating it.*

ADAM

(grabbing the Bible)

No!

STEVE

I'm starving!

ADAM

So—does everybody hate me?

STEVE

(after a beat, opening his arms, so that ADAM *can lie beside him)*

No. Never.

JANE

(still lying down, without moving)

I hate you.

ADAM

(noticing something in the sky)

Look! I feel like—singing. So the moon will know we're here.

MABEL

(singing, in a high, screechy voice, with more yearning and emotion than melody or pitch)

Hello, moon! We're down here! We love you! Especially Mabel!

EVERYONE

(joining in, using high screechy voices to imitate MABEL*'s song)*

HELLO, MOON! WE'RE DOWN HERE! WE LOVE YOU!

JANE

(singing, with gusto)

AND ADAM IS AN IDIOT WHO RUINED EVERYTHING!

EVERYONE

AND ADAM IS AN IDIOT WHO RUINED EVERYTHING!

ADAM

(Sung in a tentative, apologetic, high-pitched voice)

By accident!

EVERYONE

(continuing to sing, even louder and more atrociously)

HELLO, MOON . . .

STAGE MANAGER

(Interrupting, as they sing)

Lights sixty-four, go. Fast!

The lights go to black.

MABEL

(from the darkness, indignant)

Hey!

ADAM, STEVE, JANE, *and* MABEL *exit in the darkness. The lights come up on the* STAGE MANAGER, *crossing the stage, carrying a piece of crude, Western-style wooden fence. She speaks as she walks, eventually depositing the fence somewhere across the stage.*

STAGE MANAGER

Crude implements, go. Division of labor, go. Fence posts, go. Harvest, go. Ethnic jewelry, go.

(She has deposited the fence. As she crosses back to her desk, she spots an offensive garment on someone in the audience; she points to that audience member)

That shirt, no. Hoe-down, go. Yee-ha, go.

Some extremely sprightly music begins, perhaps the high-stepping Aaron Copland score for Rodeo. *Lights up on the full stage, which has become a bit more sunny and welcoming. The landscape, while remaining Biblical and barren, has a hint of Midwestern, pioneer spirit.*

ADAM *leaps onstage, wearing roughhewn clothing, crudely hand-stitched. He carries a crude ax. He holds out his ax to the audience; he loves his ax. He begins to dance with his ax, in a high-spirited, klutzy version of a number from* Seven Brides for Seven Brothers *or* Oklahoma. JANE *enters; she looks disgusted with* ADAM*'s dance.* ADAM *dances over to her, pauses, and then hands her the ax. She takes it, puts it over her shoulder and exits.* ADAM *is thrilled, because* JANE *will be the one to actually chop the wood; he dances offstage in the opposite direction, leaping and clicking his heels.*

As ADAM *has been dancing,* STEVE *has entered far upstage, with a bow and arrow, stalking some unseen, small animal. He also wears a new, rough-hewn outfit.* MABEL *follows close behind him, watching his every move. She wears a new dress, perhaps with long, fluid, macramé accents.*

As ADAM *dances and deals with* JANE, STEVE *and* MABEL *execute a full-stage cross. The dance,* JANE*'s entrance, and* STEVE *and* MABEL*'s hunting cross should be choreographed to happen together, for a feeling of simultaneous action.*

As ADAM *exits,* STEVE *heads downstage, stalking something.*

STEVE

(to MABEL*)*

Shh . . .

MABEL

Shh . . .

STEVE

(whispering intensely)

We must move very slowly, and we make no sudden moves, and then . . .

As STEVE *draws back his bow,* MABEL *leaps out from behind him, to warn his prey.*

MABEL

(to the animal)

Run, little one. Fear the white man!

If STEVE *is being played by a non-white actor,* MABEL*'s line should read "Run, little one! Warn the others!"*

STEVE

(furious)

Mabel!

MABEL

How would you like it if someone did that to you?

MABEL *grabs* STEVE*'s arrow and pricks his arm.*

STEVE

Oww! That hurt!

MABEL

You see? That felt—strangely arousing . . .

STEVE

Exactly! When I see these creatures, I feel this urge. To chase! To pounce! To kill!

MABEL

Let's talk about that.

STEVE

It's the natural order!

MABEL

It's evil!

STEVE

What?

MABEL

It's the opposite of goodness. Goodness is bunnies and caring and respect for all living things.

STEVE

And evil?

MABEL

(brightly, as she and STEVE *exit together)*

Evil is anything I don't like!

As MABEL *and* STEVE *exit, Jane enters, carrying a crude shovel. She stands near the fence posts. She calls out:*

JANE

Adam!

STAGE MANAGER

Laundry, go.

A clothesline appears, with some primitive burlap clothes and a muslin sheet pinned up. Adam enters, with a basket, and starts taking down the laundry.

ADAM

Jane?

JANE

I need a hand, with these fence posts.

ADAM

Fence posts? Well, if you'll help me, with the laundry.

JANE

Shit.

Jane drops her shovel, and might belch. She pulls a sheet off the clothesline and starts bunching it up; laundry is not her area of expertise.

ADAM

(*horrified*)

Jane!

JANE

What? What'd I do?

ADAM

We do not grab and bunch!

JANE

We don't?

ADAM

We fluff and fold!

ADAM *begins demonstrating correct laundry behavior, as he and* JANE *fold the sheet.*

JANE

Okay . . .

ADAM

Jane, can I ask you a personal question?

JANE

Like what?

ADAM

When you and Mabel are alone together, and you take off all of your clothes, just what exactly do the two of you sort of—do?

JANE

Do? Well, first I might take my tongue . . .

ADAM

(interrupting, running to the other side of the clothesline, terrified)

No! Stop!

JANE

Why?

ADAM

No, I can do this, keep going, tell me the whole thing . . .

JANE

(very matter-of-fact)

So I take my tongue, and I lick her eyeball. I suck it out of her head, chew on it, roll it in the dirt, then I rub the eyeball on my butt, oh, and then we both come.

ADAM

(proud of himself, for taking it well)

Okay. We should try that.

JANE

Adam! For cryin' out loud!

ADAM

What?

JANE

That isn't what we do. We kiss and suck and lick and finger and have a great time, just like you and Steve! And we're not grossed out by what you do with your fleshy little things.

ADAM

They are not little! Mine isn't.

JANE

(after a beat)

There are only two of you in the whole world, and you're comparing?

ADAM

We're both huge, and you're just jealous because you wish you had a fleshy humongous thing!

JANE

What would I do with it? Mix drinks?

ADAM

You'd be proud of it!

JANE

Adam, if we're going to create the world, we have to respect our differences.

ADAM

But why? Why are we all so different? What do you do, when it all starts to overwhelm you, and you can't sleep and you stand outside, asking and needing and crying out to the stars?

MABEL *enters, from the opposite side of the stage, looking into the cosmos.*

MABEL

Stars!

STAGE MANAGER

Stars, go. Midnight, go. Crickets, go.

The lights change dramatically, for a feeling of enchanted midnight, beneath a full moon. JANE *exits, with the laundry.* MABEL *glides into a circle of moonlight, enraptured, conducting a private ritual.*

STAGE MANAGER

Dance of the pagan earth goddess, go.

Music begins, mostly primitive but alluring rhythmic sounds, which will grow in intensity as the scene progresses. MABEL *begins to dance, her arms flung wide, as* ADAM *watches her, from behind a tree. The* STAGE MANAGER *circles* MABEL, *cueing her dance.*

STAGE MANAGER

Spirit of the forest, go. Full moon, go. Isadora Duncan, go.

(MABEL *dances with fluid, trailing, Duncan-style moves.)*

Martha Graham, go.

(MABEL'*s dance becomes abrupt and angular, in Martha Graham style.)*

Stevie Nicks, go.

(MABEL *starts to spin in a witchy, airy-fairy manner, pointing at the audience, à la Stevie Nicks in concert.)*

Interloper, go.

MABEL *pauses, realizing that* ADAM *is watching her.* ADAM *approaches* MABEL, *holding out his Bible.*

STAGE MANAGER

That thing, go.

ADAM *and* MABEL *both touch the Bible, and raise their free hands, mirroring each other.*

STAGE MANAGER

Kindred spirits, go.

ADAM *and* MABEL *take each other's crossed hands, and begin to dance, spinning together. The music grows wilder and more pounding, and the dance becomes increasingly passionate and out of control, in pagan ecstasy.*

STAGE MANAGER

(as the dance builds)

Giddy high spirits, go. Dizziness, go. Loss of self, go. Lack of oxygen, go. Sparks of blinding white light, go.

STAGE MANAGER

MABEL *and* ADAM *have been spinning wildly and independently.* MABEL *falls to her knees, overcome.*

STAGE MANAGER

Possible existence of God . . .

The Stage Manager leans down and kisses MABEL. *Then she stands back, with a certain satisfied swagger.*

STAGE MANAGER

Go.

MABEL *has felt the kiss, but she has not seen the* STAGE MANAGER. *She has experienced a form of wondrous revelation.* ADAM *watches her.*

MABEL

(reaching upward)

Oh my—God.

ADAM

God?

STAGE MANAGER

Dance of the divine, go.

The music grows even more frenzied, and ADAM *and* MABEL *resume dancing, leaping into the air with cries of joy. They dance offstage, to opposite sides. The* STAGE MANAGER *remains at center stage.*

STAGE MANAGER

Lights sixty-five, go.

The lights change, from midnight in the clearing to something brighter and domestic. The STAGE CREW *brings out a pair of benches, a fur rug, a floor lamp, and a tray holding four primitive goblets. They create* ADAM *and* STEVE'S *house, as the* STAGE MANAGER *supervises their placement of each item.*

STAGE MANAGER

Stage crew, go. Adam and Steve's house, go. Seating, go. Floor lamp, go. Area rug, go. Stemware, go.

The STAGE CREW *exits, as the* STAGE MANAGER *surveys the premises, satisfied.*

STAGE MANAGER

Early Ikea, go.

STEVE *enters, wearing fresh white linen clothing, very loose and flowing, but more tailored than his earlier outfits. He carries a tray of hors d'oeuvres.*

STEVE

They're gonna be here any minute!

ADAM *enters, also in fresh linen clothing, very excited.*

ADAM

You look so handsome.

STEVE

(proudly)

I know.

ADAM

I just want everything to be perfect!

STEVE

But why? What's going on?

ADAM

It told you, it's a surprise. The best one ever!

MABEL

(entering)

Knock, knock!

JANE

(following MABEL *onstage)*

We're here!

JANE *and* MABEL *enter, carrying a bottle of wine; they also wear white linen outfits.* JANE*'s look will always be a variation on overalls, for practicality.* MABEL*'s outfits will always be more flowing and romantic. The foursome greet each other very socially, with hugs and air-kisses. They have all clearly become experts at brunch behavior.*

ADAM

Jane!

STEVE

Mabel!

MABEL

We brought you something!

JANE *or* MABEL *hand* STEVE *the bottle of wine.*

STEVE

Wine!

JANE

We made it, from our own grapes.

STEVE

(reading the label on the bottle, impressed)

"Jane and Mabel. Monday."

ADAM

Come in, sit down.

STEVE

(holding the tray of hors d'oeuvres)

Can I offer anyone some of these things that Adam made?

JANE

What are they?

ADAM

Well, I had this idea. What if, before the actual meal, we all got to taste some smaller, more complicated food.

MABEL

But—we already do that.

ADAM

(his trump card)

On a cracker?

Everyone goes "Oooh!", tasting the hors d'oeuvres, impressed at ADAM'S *innovation.*

ADAM

(as he pours wine into the goblets and distributes them)

Now, after the garden, I know that we all thought that maybe—we weren't going to make it. That because of what I did . . .

(everyone protests vigorously—"No, no!" "Leave it alone!" "It was ages ago!" etc.)

No no no no no, that because of my wanting a revelation, we were doomed. But as of today, we have all been together for 400 years. And I think we look great!

Everyone raises their goblets and agrees, in a wholehearted group toast:

JANE: Yes to that!
STEVE: Here, here!
ADAM: Way to go!
MABEL: Rock on!

(all at the same time)

ADAM

And I would just like to mention some of the wonderful things we have invented, including the lever, the pulley system, and the wheel.

STEVE

(toasting JANE *and* MABEL, *with great respect)*

Thank you, ladies.

MABEL

And let's not forget about shampoo and conditioner in one!

JANE

(with respect)

Adam.

Everyone toasts ADAM, *who holds up his hands—"What can I say?"*

ADAM

And yet—our happiness hasn't been complete. We have each other, we have so much, but still—we know nothing. We have no answers. Until—right now!

STEVE

Is this your surprise?

JANE

What? What is this?

ADAM

Mabel?

MABEL

(standing, with a real sense of the momentous occasion)

All right. Well, last night, I—made contact.

STEVE

Contact?

MABEL

We were out dancing, and the sky was so clear, and the stars were so bold, and I just wanted to reach out and say, I love everything!

STEVE

(amused)

Mabel.

JANE

Mushrooms?

MABEL

No! And as I raised my arms, to embrace the universe, I felt—a kiss.

JANE

A kiss?

MABEL

And I opened my eyes, and I said, "Oh my *God.*"

ADAM

She did. I heard it!

STEVE

God?

JANE

God?

MABEL

God is—this is so cool—the creator of the cosmos, and the source of all spiritual and moral nourishment.

ADAM *looks at* STEVE *and* JANE*; he is very impressed with* MABEL*'s story.* JANE *and* STEVE *exchange a glance.*

JANE

Too much free time.

STEVE

Let's eat.

JANE *and* STEVE *stand and begin to leave.*

ADAM

You guys! It really happened!

MABEL

And we think that all of God's teachings may be in this.

ADAM *holds up his Bible.*

JANE

An object which makes no sense.

ADAM

Not yet.

STEVE

Mabel, I love you, and Adam, I know you ask questions, but guys—this is the most dangerous idea I have ever heard.

ADAM

Why?

STEVE

Because we have all worked very hard. To grow food, to build our homes. To create a casual yet elegant lifestyle. And now you want to take that away, to say, oh no, something called God did it?

MABEL

That's not what we're saying.

STEVE

(to MABEL*)*

If any of this nonsense is true, then how come you're the only one who really made contact?

MABEL

That's fair. And I've thought about it. Okay. Now if you had to choose someone from among, say, the four of us, someone to receive a vision of spiritual wonder, now whom would you pick?

(looking around the room)

Hmmm. Well, it wouldn't be Adam, because he's so sweet, but he isn't exactly stable.

ADAM

I'm not?

MABEL

(sitting on the bench beside ADAM *and taking his hand; she speaks to him in a totally sweet and sympathetic manner)*

One word, sweetie: "garden"?

(She chortles adorably, tweaks ADAM*'s nose or shakes a you-naughty-boy finger at him. Then she glides over to* STEVE*)*

And Steve, you're so hard-working and clear-eyed, only you lack any imagination or a larger sense of life.

(She says this without a trace of rancor, as if it's the best compliment)

Not that that's a bad thing. Necessarily.

(After patting STEVE*'s chest, she goes to* JANE*, and puts her arms around her, speaking in the warmest, most loving tone imaginable)*

And of course I adore Jane, but she's still in recovery.

STEVE

In recovery? From what?

JANE

These conversations.

MABEL

And I'm, well, I'm open and sensitive and more highly evolved. And I have the best hair.

ADAM, JANE, AND STEVE

(vehemently)

You do not!

MABEL

People? So, God chose me. It's no big deal.

STEVE

Wait. Mabel?

MABEL

Yes?

STEVE

I'm not judging, but—is this some sort of women's thing?

JANE

Excuse me?

STEVE

You know, like making tea from bark and keeping a journal and inventing those big, ugly brown sandals?

JANE

(who's wearing those sandals)

They're very comfortable!

STEVE

For evening?

ADAM

Steve!

MABEL

Let's all join hands and offer ourselves to God!

ADAM

We could try! This is so exciting!

JANE

Maybe after dinner.

STEVE

Not in my house.

ADAM

Your house?

STEVE

I will not believe in something I can't see or smell or touch.

ADAM

You believe in love.

STEVE

Not at the moment.

MABEL

You love Adam. God made Adam. So you should thank God. You should show God you're grateful.

STEVE

Grateful? I'm sorry, but I will not suck up to some invisible, nonexistent being!

ADAM

Wait! Be careful! What if God, okay, what if something as powerful as God, heard what you just said and got angry?

STEVE

I don't care!

MABEL

Don't say that!

JANE

I know—let's invent Charades!

STEVE

We are not going to be punished for having a conversation! What are you so afraid of?

MABEL

The wrath of God!

STEVE

There is no God!

STAGE MANAGER

Flood, go.

There is a huge clap of thunder, and suddenly the stage goes black. A torrential rain is heard.

ADAM

Just for the record—that was Steve!

STAGE MANAGER

El Niño, go.

More thunder is heard, and the rain gets even heavier. ADAM, STEVE, JANE, *and* MABEL *exit, as the* STAGE CREW, *led by the* STAGE MANAGER, *pulls billowing yards of blue silk across the entire stage, as the flood. The* STAGE MANAGER *and her* CREW *all wear bright yellow rain slickers and matching hats. Booming, urgent, movie-style hurricane music is heard.*

STAGE MANAGER

Ark, go, surviving creatures, go. Two by two, go.

During these cues our foursome make a full-stage cross, fighting the gale-force winds and rain, making their way onto the ark, as we hear the sounds of a ship's whistle amid the music and hurricane din. The group might wear rainwear; JANE *carries a duffel bag,* MABEL *carries a guitar case with floral decals,* STEVE *carries the floor lamp over his head, and* ADAM *carries his Bible and a garment bag. As our foursome make their cross and exit, they are followed by two actors dressed as* RABBITS. *The*

RABBITS have big floppy ears and cottontails, and also wear brightly colored, touristy sportswear, including Bermuda shorts, Hawaiian shirts, day-glo fanny packs, etc. Before exiting, the RABBITS pause briefly. They are thrilled to be going on a cruise: RABBIT #1 poses, while RABBIT #2 snaps his picture with a Kodak Instamatic, including a flash. Then the RABBITS hurry offstage, making a brief hop in unison. Various scenic pieces can also be brought onstage during all of this hubbub. They include a ship's bar and a section of railing. The benches from ADAM and STEVE's house can be rearranged to form a straight line upstage center.

STAGE MANAGER

Promenade deck, go. Contents of Adam's stomach, go.

Lights up on a section of railing, with a life preserver. ADAM runs on and leans over the railing. He almost vomits, but doesn't. STEVE runs on after ADAM, concerned.

STEVE

Are you okay?

ADAM

Make it stop! The rain. The flood.

STEVE

How?

ADAM

(holding out his Bible)

Ask God! Tell God you're sorry!

STEVE

Why?

STAGE MANAGER

Thunderbolt, go.

A bolt of lightening pierces the sky; it is very frightening.

STEVE

Okay, fine, I'll try!

ADAM hands STEVE the Bible; STEVE stands at the railing and addresses God, looking upward.

STEVE

God, even though you're just one of Mabel's spinning-induced hallucinations, and this is totally stupid, I'm really sorry, so stop the flood. Thank you.

ADAM

Steve.

STEVE

What?

ADAM

Nice try! Do you think God is gonna hear that? And pay attention? Say you're sorry!

ADAM *gestures to God, regarding* STEVE—*"I don't know what he's thinking."* STEVE *leans at the railing and tries again, with more fervent intensity. Adam stands behind him, acting as a coach.*

STEVE

God . . .

ADAM

Be charming.

STEVE

(in a deep, almost English voice, to God)

My darling . . .

ADAM

Be respectful!

STEVE

My Lord . . .

ADAM

Get chummy!

STEVE

Lookin' good!

ADAM

Pour it on!

STEVE

I love your work!

ADAM

You are *hot.*

STEVE

You are *hot.*

ADAM

You are *it!*

STEVE

You are *it!*

ADAM

Oh, you big damn juicy God baby . . .

STEVE

Oh, you big damn juicy—

(still to God)

Can I ask you something?

ADAM

What?

STEVE

(to God)

If you made everything, then who made you?

We hear a thunderclap.

ADAM

(to God)

Not an issue!

STEVE

(to God)

And if you're so wonderful, then why are we afraid of you?

Another thunderclap, even louder.

ADAM

(to God, regarding STEVE*)*

Don't listen!

STEVE

(turning to ADAM*)*

Adam, do you love God?

ADAM

Of course!

STEVE

More than you love me?

A thunder crash, as ADAM *and* STEVE *stare at each other. Lights down on the railing, as* ADAM *and* STEVE *exit, perhaps taking the railing with them.*

STAGE MANAGER

Mid-Atlantic, go.

Lights up on the ark dining room. This may be suggested simply by having JANE *and* MABEL *sitting beside each other on a bench. Their body language tells us that all is not well between them;* JANE *is sipping from a flask. They have just finished a meal, in silence.* MABEL *waves to someone across the room.*

MABEL

Hi!

MABEL *barks like a dog, loud and sharp. Then, acknowledging another friend, she snorts noisily, like a pig. Spotting a third friend, she quacks like a duck or squawks like a chicken.*

JANE

(barely controlling herself)

Could you please not do that?

MABEL

Do what?

JANE

Make animal noises, at dinner.

MABEL

Well, I have to talk to someone.

JANE

Meaning?

MABEL

We haven't spoken for the last two weeks.

JANE

So what's there to talk about? "Hey, you think it's gonna *rain?*"

MABEL

We're a couple, we're not supposed to run out of things to say!

JANE

It's been *four hundred years.*

(she sips from the flask)

And thirty-nine days . . .

MABEL

It's just that sometimes . . .

JANE

Sometimes what?

MABEL

(getting increasingly shrill)

Nothing! I love you! It's just that sometimes I can't stand you!

JANE

Well, I love you too, but if I hear that whiny little baby-talk voice one more time, I'm gonna scream!

Sexy, mambo music is heard. FLUFFY, *an extremely sexual cat, enters, clearly on the prowl.* FLUFFY *walks upright, and her costume might include elements of human attire, but she is immediately recognizable as a cat—she has whiskers, pointy ears, paws, and a tail. She purrs her way over toward* JANE *and* MABEL, *heating up the atmosphere considerably.*

FLUFFY

Hi, Jane.

MABEL

Jane?

JANE

(aroused)

Hey there, Fluffy.

MABEL

Fluffy?

FLUFFY

(joining them on the bench, getting physical)

And this must be Mabel. I've heard so much about you.

MABEL

How?

JANE

We met last night, after you fell asleep.

MABEL

(to JANE*)*

You went out?

FLUFFY

Heavy petting.

JANE

(to FLUFFY*)*

So where's your better half?

BABE, *a pig, enters.* BABE *is a lusty, life-of-the-party pig, a sexually voracious, good-time sow. Her personality combines elements of a frat guy and a Shriner out for a wild night on the town. She also walks upright, but is pure pig; she has pig ears, a sizable snout, and a curly tail.*

BABE

Jane!

FLUFFY

(to BABE*)*

Sweetheart!

MABEL

Jane?

BABE

(offering her hoof, introducing herself to MABEL*)*

Babe.

FLUFFY

All the animals are mixing.

BABE

(who has joined the others on the bench, nuzzling with FLUFFY*)*

Last night, we had sex with a goldfish.

MABEL

A goldfish?

BABE

She died happy!

FLUFFY

But this is so much better.

MABEL

But I don't think that females really enjoy open relationships. Women are naturally monogamous.

BABE

You really think so?

MABEL

Of course!

JANE

(standing, eyeballing BABE *lasciviously)*

Oink.

FLUFFY *grabs* MABEL *and kisses her passionately.*

BABE

(swaggering, to JANE*)*

I should warn you—I'm Canadian.

FLUFFY

(breaking the kiss)

What's wrong—cat got your tongue?

MABEL

No!

FLUFFY

I know that you're scared, so was I, my first time . . .

BABE

(to MABEL*)*

What's wrong? You kosher?

MABEL

No . . .

JANE

(to MABEL*)*

You always say we should be open to new experiences . . .

MABEL

(increasingly panicked)

But—with animals?

BABE

(very offended)

Hey! What's wrong with animals?

MABEL

Nothing! I love animals!

FLUFFY

Prove it!

FLUFFY *lets loose with a shrieking, passionate meow, whips the bench with her tail, and chases* MABEL *offstage.*

MABEL

(on her way out, desperately)

Jane!

JANE

(totally up for sex, as a lusty love call, to BABE*)*

Soo-eee!

BABE

(as Jane exits, following Fluffy and Mabel:)

That's right, baby! Try the other white meat!

Babe exits, in heat.

STAGE MANAGER

Admiral's Club, go.

Loud, thumping disco music begins. Steve enters, in a rage, and heads for the bar. The BARTENDER *turns around—he is a* RHINO. *He is very sexy, perhaps shirtless or wearing a leather vest over his bare skin. He has an enormous, rough horn in the middle of his face, at least 15".*

STEVE

Gimme a beer!

RHINO

(handing him a beer)

Here you go.

STEVE

(explosive)

Have you ever been in love?

RHINO

Sure!

STEVE

I hate it! Everything's all my fault! There's just mildew and sulking and animals!

RHINO

You know who I was in love with?

STEVE

Who? What?

RHINO

(gesturing)

Over there, by the door. Simba.

STEVE

Simba?

RHINO

They call him the Lion King. I don't think so.

STEVE

Really?

RHINO

I found out, he was fucking everything on this boat. Dumbo. Daffy. Goofy came to me in tears. He said, all Simba wants is a big career in show business. And now I guess he's gonna get it. See who he's with?

STEVE

(looking across the room)

You're kidding . . .

RHINO

That's right. Mickey! With the gloves and the buttons! Can you imagine?

(in a high-pitched Mickey Mouse voice)

"Oh Simba, do me!"

STEVE

You poor guy.

RHINO

We both need it bad.

STEVE

It's been weeks . . .

RHINO

You are making me so hot . . .

STEVE *and the* RHINO *have begun fondling each other.*

STEVE

(trying to break away)

But we can't . . .

RHINO

Your boyfriend doesn't know what he's got . . .

STEVE

But he's a great guy, I mean, on land . . .

RHINO

But we're not on land, we may never get back on land . . .

STEVE

We could be out here for eternity, with the water rising, and the walls closing in . . .

RHINO

With Adam telling you all about God . . .

STEVE

How can I love Adam so much, and still not push you away . . .

The RHINO *has pursued* STEVE, *stepping out from behind the bar.* STEVE *reaches out and begins to stroke the* RHINO's *horn, closing his hand around it, his strokes becoming more vigorous, as the* RHINO *moans with passion. Then* STEVE *licks his middle fingers and slaps the* RHINO's *horn, which makes the* RHINO *yelp with lust. The* RHINO *and* STEVE, *overcome by the moment, grab each other and begin kissing passionately.* ADAM *enters from the opposite side of the stage, wrapped in a blanket. When he sees* STEVE *and the* RHINO, *he is stunned, and genuinely hurt.*

ADAM

Steve?

STEVE *and the* RHINO *break apart.*

STEVE

Adam!

ADAM

No . . .

RHINO

(to ADAM*)*

Can I get you something?

STEVE

I can explain . . .

ADAM

Steve . . .

(as STEVE *approaches him)*

Get away from me!

STEVE

I was upset, I was angry . . .

RHINO

Hey, he said you were having problems . . .

ADAM

(to STEVE, *regarding the* RHINO*)*

You told him? About our personal lives?

STEVE

We *are* having problems!

ADAM

Which you won't talk about!

STEVE

We don't do anything but talk! When was the last time we had sex?

ADAM

Excuse me, I've been vomiting!

STEVE

Oh, so now who won't talk about it?

ADAM

How come this is suddenly about me? I'm the one who just walked in on you, fondling some—some butch can opener!

RHINO

A rhino! You got a problem with that?

ADAM

(to STEVE*)*

I have a problem with the fact that I loved you so much, up until thirty seconds ago. And now, for the first time, I feel so—betrayed.

MABEL

(from offstage)

No! Stop it! Leave me alone!

MABEL *runs onstage, sobbing, very upset, wrapped in a blanket.*

ADAM

Mabel?

MABEL

I'm sorry, I'm sorry, but I just can't!

MABEL *huddles on the bench, as Jane runs on, buttoning her clothes.*

JANE

That was incredibly rude!

MABEL *starts to hack and cough, making a series of horrible rasping noises, trying to get something out of her throat.*

STEVE

(regarding MABEL*'s spasm)*

What's wrong with her?

MABEL

(finally coughing something up, and looking at it, in her hand, totally grossed out)

Oh my God! It's a furball!

JANE

We were having fun!

MABEL

I wasn't! Why do you need that? Why aren't I enough?

JANE

You were there! You were part of it!

MABEL

(with volcanic fury)

She was a *PIG!*

STEVE

Mabel!

RHINO

Whoa!

JANE

In a blanket!

MABEL

It was against God's law!

JANE

It's your law!

STEVE

Why do we need laws?

MABEL

So people won't hurt each other!

ADAM

And cheat on each other!

MABEL

With sows!

ADAM

(referring to the RHINO*)*

With luggage!

FLUFFY

(from offstage)

Don't touch me!

BABE

(from offstage)

Get back here!

FLUFFY *runs on, disheveled and very upset.*

FLUFFY

It's over!

JANE

What's wrong?

FLUFFY

I can't live like this! Not anymore!

BABE *runs on and pursues* FLUFFY, *who might jump atop the bar.*

BABE

Get back to the sty!

FLUFFY

I won't. You're too exhausting!
(to the group)
She's got six nipples!

MABEL

Why can't everyone just stay together?

ADAM

The way God intended!

JANE

Because the world is more interesting than that!

STEVE

Because God is what's fucking us up!

BABE

Stop it! You're upsetting the lower primates!

We hear all the animals on the ark begin to yelp and roar.

RHINO

They're gonna stampede!

FLUFFY

(to BABE*)*
I hate you!

ADAM

(to STEVE*)*
I hate you more!

MABEL

(to JANE*)*
You've ruined everything!

JANE

(to MABEL*)*
You're insane!

STEVE

(to ADAM*)*
You're hysterical!

RHINO

Hey—it's stopped raining.

STAGE MANAGER

Sunshine, go. Blue sky, go. Rainbow, go.

Everyone stops fighting as the ark vanishes, and FLUFFY, BABE, *and the* RHINO *exit. The sky clears, and a vibrant, glowing sun appears. The ark might disappear simply by having the* STAGEHANDS *and the* STAGE MANAGER *remove the various set pieces. The action should remain continuous.*

ADAM

(pointing into the distance, toward the audience)

Look—land!

STAGE MANAGER

Dove, go.

ADAM, STEVE, JANE, *and* MABEL *all follow the path of a dove, flying high above their heads.* DAD #1 *enters. He is a wholesome, good-natured, suburban-style fellow.*

DAD #1

Hey there!

ADAM

Who . . . who are you?

MABEL

Oh my God . . .

JANE

There—there are more of us!

STAGE MANAGER

Rest of the world, go.

Through slides or a painted drop or some other scenic device, the image of thousands of other people appears, filling the stage.

ADAM

This is incredible!

STEVE

There are all these people!

MABEL

All these friends!

JANE

But where did they—where did all of you come from?

MABEL

From God!

STEVE

Let them answer!

DAD #1

We came from—across the ocean. There was a flood, which destroyed everything, but we got onboard this other ark.

JANE

Spooky . . .

DAD #1 *is joined by his wife,* MOM #1, *and another happy, heterosexual couple,* DAD #2 *and* MOM ##2. *The couples should be in no way cartoony or vicious; they are welcoming, sociable, and curious. They are dressed in a not-quite-modern-yet-suburban style, possibly all in white; their outfits might include Bermuda shorts, shirt-waist dresses and windbreakers. The two* MOMS *might wear sleek blonde pageboy hairdos, although they shouldn't match. The* MOMS *and* DADS *stay together as a group, although the couples should be very affectionate with their spouses.*

STEVE

But—there are so many of you.

MOM #1

More every day!

ADAM

But how? How did that happen? How do you . . . make more of you?

DAD #1

(very jovial)

Well, I just take my penis . . .

MOM #1

(brightly)

And he puts it in my vagina!

ADAM, STEVE, JANE, *and* MABEL *stare at the newcomers in horror and disbelief. After a beat*

ADAM, STEVE, JANE AND MABEL

GROSS!

DAD #2

(very affable)

No, really, it's great fun. I ejaculate, and then, oh, about nine months later . . .

MOM #2

A baby! Happens all the time!

ADAM, STEVE, JANE, *and* MABEL *look at each other; they are all deeply skeptical. Adam steps forward, taking command.*

ADAM

Excuse me.

DAD #1

Yes?

ADAM

Now—all right. Okay. Joke over. What you're saying, what you're claiming, is that the men—have sex—with the women?

ADAM, STEVE, JANE, *and* MABEL *burst out laughing. The heterosexuals aren't offended by this response, just politely puzzled.*

MOM #2

But we do!

DAD #1

Every chance we get!

DAD #2

Like fallin' off a log!

MOM #1

Works for us!

ADAM

Well, that is just *wrong!*

JANE

That is unnatural!

MABEL

How could there be any possible pleasure in it?

STEVE

That is just not what God intended!

Everyone stares at STEVE*; he looks around.*

STEVE

Who said that?

DAD #1

God?

MABEL

Well, with the way you behave, I'm sure you've probably never heard of God.

MOM #1

But of course we have!

DAD #1

We love God!

MOM #2

We worship God!

DAD #2

We're God's chosen people!

MOM #2

(politely, for information)

And you are . . .?

ADAM

We're—we're God's chosen people!

DAD #2

But there are so few of you. Only four.

JANE

Because we're gay!

STEVE

We don't have children!

ADAM

We have taste!

MABEL

But how can there be two different gods?

STEVE

How can there be any?

ADAM

(holding up his Bible)

But we have this! Our Bible!

DAD #1

Just like ours!

The MOMS *and* DADS *all take out their own Bibles, which are more deluxe than* ADAM*'s.*

MOM #1

(stroking her Bible's binding)

Only in leather.

ADAM

But—can you read them?

MOM #1

Of course! Every day!

ADAM

But—what do they say?

DAD #2

(opening his Bible)

Well . . .

MOM #2

(opening her Bible)

Let's take a look . . .

DAD #1

(pointing to a passage)

Oh, I love this . . .

MOM #1

(pointing to another passage)

No, honey, here . . .

From offstage, we hear a baby cry.

DAD #1

Uh-oh!

JANE

What was that?

MOM #2

That's the new baby! He's hungry!

We hear more babies begin to cry.

DAD #1

We better get busy!

Even more babies begin to cry, and we hear older children calling out "Mommy!" and "Daddy!"

MOM #1

We've got to run! You understand. Nice to meet you.

DAD #1

We'll get together! When we can find a sitter!

MOM #2

Call us!

DAD #1

We mean it!

DAD #2

I bet you'll all make great aunts and uncles!

MOM #1

And—entertainers!

MOMS AND DADS

Bye!

The four straight people run off. ADAM, STEVE, JANE, *and* MABEL *stare at each other, trying to process what they've just seen and heard.*

ADAM

What was *that?*

JANE

The world is getting very strange . . .

STEVE

So, do you still believe in God? After all that?

MABEL

Yes.

STEVE

Mabel!

MABEL

And I think that God—is trying to teach us something.

ADAM

Teach us what?

MABEL

I don't know. Maybe something about—babies.

(gazing offstage)

Look at them—they're like teeny, tiny little people. Like lawn ornaments.

JANE

They're so noisy, and smelly.

STEVE

What if those people move near us, with all those children?

MABEL

(turning to JANE, *with great, yearning determination)*

I want one!

JANE

You do not!

MABEL

I want another one of us! Of you and me!

JANE

Well, I don't think that's gonna happen! Didn't you hear what you have to do to get one of those?

*(*STEVE *turns to* STEVE*)*

MABEL

Steve?

STEVE

What?

MABEL

(seductively)

Steve?

MABEL *flips her hair flirtatiously and walks over to* STEVE, *with her version of a sexy walk. Somewhat awkwardly,* MABEL *and* STEVE *kiss.* ADAM *and* JANE *watch them, as the kiss grows more intense. Finally,* MABEL *and* STEVE *break the kiss.*

MABEL

Why . . . why did I just feel this huge drop in my self-esteem?

JANE

You see what happens?

ADAM

But those babies are really adorable . . .

STEVE

Adam?

MABEL

Adam?

ADAM

I'm not saying it's a good idea, but—what if it is? Wouldn't that be amazing? A little Adam running around? We could do things with him, guy things!

JANE

Guy things?

ADAM

Like cooking, and skincare, and the theater!

STEVE

But what if the baby's a girl?

ADAM

We could try again.

MABEL

Adam!

ADAM

(to the women)

Or we could give her to you.

JANE

Hold it! If God wants any of us to have a baby, well, we can just do it the right way!

MABEL

How?

JANE

(gesturing to the offstage people)

We can steal one!

STEVE

How can you all talk about having babies together, and what God wants? Weren't you on that ark? When we were all ready to kill each other?

JANE

When we learned a little too much?

ADAM

That's right. What about—us?

MABEL

Us?

ADAM

Does God want us to stay together?

STEVE

Do *we* want to?

The foursome are not just referring to the relationships of the two couples, but to the group as a whole. The foursome is at a crisis point, on every level.

MABEL

We need to talk, before we go any further. We need some rules.

JANE

No more rules!

ADAM

What if we have a baby, and the baby asks—where did I come from? Who made me?

PHARAOH'S VOICE

(boomingly amplified, so it resounds throughout the theater)

I AM THE ONE TRUE GOD!

JANE

(looking around)

What the fuck was that?

PHARAOH'S VOICE

I AM IMMORTAL.

STEVE

Don't listen!

PHARAOH'S VOICE

COME UNTO ME!

FTATATEETA, *a female Egyptian guard, appears wearing a headdress, armor, a pleated white skirt, lace-up sandals, and Cleopatra eyeliner. She carries a spear. She marches downstage center and assumes an Egyptian pose. She has the attitude of a gum-chewing waitress in a spotlight.*

FTATATEETA

Welcome—to the grand imperial court of Raman-hotep, beloved Pharaoh of all Egypt.

STAGE MANAGER

All Egypt, go.

Grand, booming, Ten-Commandments-style imperial music is heard, and ancient Egypt appears. The atmosphere should suggest Egypt by way of the MGM Luxor Hotel in Las Vegas, with an emphasis on gold draperies, boldly colored hieroglyphs, palm fronds, and perhaps some pyramids and a sphinx. PEGGY, *a second female guard in an identical outfit, also with a spear, joins* FTATATEETA. *Finally, the* PHARAOH *is brought forth, as the music peaks; he might be wheeled on inside a pyramid or arrayed on a garish, ornamental throne. He rises, and strides forward, displaying his magnificence. His striped headdress and flowing, glittering robes are reminiscent of the blindingly golden attire of Tutankhamen, by way of Ziegfeld. His eyes are made up Cleopatra-style. He holds out his arms, his pleated cape billowing majestically. He is truly regal, convinced of his own godhead.*

PHARAOH

(referring to his outfit)

Too busy?

FTATATEETA

All hail Egypt's immortal Boy-King!

PEGGY

Bow down!

The guards threaten ADAM, STEVE, JANE, *and* MABEL *with their spears, and the foursome kneel on the ground.*

PHARAOH

You are surrounded by my ferocious Amazon guards. They are lesbians, trained in the deadly arts of torture, gouging, and intramural field hockey.

PHARAOH

PEGGY *and* FTATATEETA, *stationed on either side of the Pharaoh's throne, execute identical, crisp field hockey moves with their spears, thwacking imaginary pucks.*

May I present—Ftatateeta.

FTATATEETA *and* PEGGY *have resumed their military positions beside the throne.*

FTATATEETA

Yo!

PHARAOH

And—Peggy.

PEGGY

Hi, everybody!

PHARAOH

I have enslaved hundreds of thousands of homosexuals, to build my pyramids.

(He steps forward, looking into the audience)

Oh, look at them all, just sitting there.

(a beat)

Criticizing.

(in a whiny voice)

"Why can't we build a beach house?"

(in imperial tones)

Get to work!

ADAM

Your Highness?

PHARAOH

Who speaks?

ADAM

Are you really—God?

PHARAOH

(referring to himself)

Behold!

ADAM

Did you create the world?

PHARAOH

Ask anyone!

ADAM

Did you create—me?

PHARAOH

You, you, you, it's all about you!

ADAM

Did you?

PHARAOH

I suppose. Why are you questioning me?

ADAM

Because, if you're the ultimate supreme being, then this is the most important day of our lives, and our quest is ended. But it's just, if you're really God . . .

PHARAOH

Yes?

ADAM

Then why are you wearing so much eye makeup?

FTATATEETA

(threatening ADAM *with her spear)*

Silence!

PHARAOH

(striding over to ADAM, *after a beat)*

Bitch!

ADAM

And why have you brought us here before you?

PHARAOH

Because—I grieve.

ADAM

Your Highness?

PHARAOH

I am—in love.

JANE

Watch out.

STEVE

(to the PHARAOH*)*

Whom are you in love with?

PHARAOH

I found him many years ago, in the bulrushes.

ADAM

After work?

PHARAOH

(after swivelling to glare at ADAM*)*

He was floating, in a crude wooden cradle. I had never glimpsed such a beautiful child. I decreed, let him be raised in my palace, as a prince!

MABEL

What did you call him?

PHARAOH

(proudly)

Brad.

JANE

Brad?

PHARAOH

It means, "He who never wishes to work."

ADAM

And what happened?

PHARAOH

We laughed together, played together, we shared every Egyptian interest—slavery, sand, sketching each other in profile. And soon, he grew to boyhood, and then, all too quickly, he became a young man. I questioned our relationship—were we friends, brothers, immortal Boy-King and grateful swamp Jew? And lo, one evening he came unto me. I pushed him away, I said I shall not have this, you must not feel this is demanded of you.

ADAM

And he said . . .?

PHARAOH

He protested, he wept, he said, yes, you are immortal, yes, you command all Egypt, and yes, I am but Brad of the bulrushes . . .

During the PHARAOH*'s last speech,* BRAD *has entered, staring passionately at the* PHARAOH. BRAD *is a handsome, well-built young fellow, wearing a white pleated skirt, a yarmulke with a bobby pin, and a tallis, the traditional Jewish prayer shawl, over his bare chest. He is earnest and ardent.*

BRAD

(to the PHARAOH*)*

But I love thee!

PHARAOH

Brad!

BRAD

(to the group)

I love him! I call him by a special title!

ADAM

Which is?

PHARAOH

"The Mouth of the Nile."

(The PHARAOH *is thrilled and overcome by this phrase. He almost swoons, then pulls himself together, and turns to* JANE *and* MABEL.*)*

Could you die?

BRAD

But he's afraid! He hesitates! He will not commit!

ADAM

But why not?

PHARAOH

Because I am immortal—but is our love?

JANE

What?

PHARAOH

I have had all of you captured for this very reason. I am told that you have loved, in a time before time. That yours were the first loves on Earth. So I must know, you must answer the legendary riddle of the Sphinx: Can love endure?

BRAD

Answer, I beseech thee!

BRAD *is now posed becomingly at the* PHARAOH*'s feet.*

PHARAOH

(with a grand gesture)

Approach, lesbians!

JANE *and* MABEL *stand.*

PHARAOH

Guards—slay the younger!

MABEL *is hurled to the ground, and* FTATATEETA *holds her spear at* MABEL*'s throat.* PEGGY *keeps* JANE *at bay with her spear.* ADAM, STEVE, JANE, *and* MABEL *all cry out; there should be a real sense of life-and-death danger.*

JANE

No!

MABEL

(to the PHARAOH*)*

You are not God, mister! I will call upon the true God to smite you!

PHARAOH

The true God?

MABEL

Dear Lord in heaven—smite him!

Everyone onstage looks to heaven—nothing happens. Everyone looks back to MABEL.

PHARAOH

Yes, dear?

MABEL

(to heaven)

Smite him eventually!

JANE

Leave her alone!

MABEL

Jane?

PHARAOH

Answer the riddle—would you die for this woman?

ADAM

Jane?

STEVE

Jane?

Everyone onstage turns to JANE. JANE *has her hands raised, the spear at her throat. She speaks with passion and fury.*

JANE

Yes, I would die for her!

MABEL

You would?

JANE

She's insane, and she tries to find higher meaning in just about everything, and she's nowhere near as open and free as she thinks she is, and I'm totally split on the God thing, let alone the baby thing, but if anyone gets to kill her—it should be me!

MABEL

(overwhelmed)

Jane!

PHARAOH

(to the guards, regarding MABEL*)*

Release her! Threaten the males!

The guards release JANE *and* MABEL, *who embrace.* FTATATEETA *puts her spear to* ADAM*'s throat, while* PEGGY *keeps Steve at bay with her spear. Everyone screams.*

PHARAOH

(to ADAM*)*

Would you die for this man?

ADAM

Yes!

PHARAOH

So you love him forever?

ADAM

I . . . I did.

STEVE

You—did?

ADAM

In the garden. When there were only the two of us. When we had no choice.

STEVE

We always had a choice.

PHARAOH

And now?

ADAM

The world has become enormous. There are so many people.

STEVE

They don't matter! We don't have to listen to them!

ADAM

But I want to listen, I need to. That's what you don't understand. You won't ask questions. You won't even ask directions.

STEVE

Why should I?

ADAM

(genuinely being torn apart)

You see? That's what drives me crazy! You are so sure of yourself, of everything, which is what I love about you, that strength, but it's also what I hate! Half the time I want you so bad I ache from it, and half the time I want to throw you off a cliff!

STEVE

That's what love is!

ADAM

Which part?

STEVE

(with equal fervor)

All of it! I love you because you're passionate and eager and optimistic, and because you're a total mess!

ADAM

But—you have been with other men!

STEVE

I have not!

ADAM

On the ark!

STEVE

That was a rhinoceros!

PHARAOH

(After a beat, he raises his arms, and all but swoons again, trying to picture this rhino moment)

A—rhinoceros?

STEVE

(to ADAM*)*

And what about you and your little Bible? You haven't exactly been a picnic!

ADAM

Oh yes I have!

STEVE

Who got us thrown out of the garden?

ADAM

Into the world!

STEVE

Which has caused all of our problems!

ADAM

Yeah, well, who started the flood that drowned just about everything?

STEVE

That wasn't my fault! I just said that I didn't believe in God!

JANE

Here we go!

PHARAOH

You don't believe in me?

MABEL

(to the PHARAOH*)*

You're not God!

STEVE

There is no God!

BRAD

Wait!

(to the PHARAOH*)*

You lied to me! You said that you were God!

PHARAOH

I am God!

BRAD

Not according to these people!

(to the foursome)

He never lets me meet anyone!

BRAD, *in a major snit, strides over to the Pharaoh's throne and sits, crossing his legs.*

PHARAOH

Excuse me! I give you gold ornaments, I dress you in precious silks!

BRAD

Last year's!

JANE

(to BRAD, *regarding the Pharaoh)*

He's a rotten boyfriend!

STEVE

(to BRAD*)*

You can do better!

BRAD

You know it! You've been there! You've been taken for granted!

PHARAOH

(to BRAD*)*

You are listening to someone who fucked a rhinoceros!

ADAM

That's right. All right, let's get it all out in the open. Steve, you just have problems because I'm the butch one.

STEVE

(incredulous)

You're the butch one?

MABEL

Why does anyone have to be the butch one?

JANE

I'm the butch one!

ADAM

(to STEVE*)*

You don't respect me, or my Bible!

PHARAOH

Your Bible?

ADAM

(examining his Bible)

It could tell me what to do! I think it holds the answers to everything!

PHARAOH

(sincerely, with great yearning)

Even—*stains?*

STEVE

Adam! I am right here, in front of you! Where I have been since the beginning! Why do you need a book, or a god, to tell you to love me? Are you that pathetic? Are you that weak?

(a beat)

ADAM

No. I am that strong. Strong enough to believe.

MABEL

Yes!

ADAM

I am leaving! I am going to lead my people into the desert!

PHARAOH

Your *people?*

ADAM

(facing the audience, addressing the hundreds of thousands of slaves)

Who wants to find a righteous way to live, in a world filled with deception?

A recorded crowd roars its approval.

ADAM

Who wants to discover the true nature of God, and the purpose of the universe?

The crowd roars even louder.

ADAM

Who wants to prove that love does not endure? Not once you leave the garden. In the world, you will be hurt. And betrayed. And you will be better off—alone.

STEVE

Is that what you believe?

ADAM

(to the crowd)

Follow me.

STEVE

Adam!

ADAM *exits, with his Bible. After a beat,* PEGGY *drops her spear and follows him. As she exits, she pauses to make a strangled cry of romantic distress.*

FTATATEETA

Peggy!

BRAD, *furious, also exits with great petulance, following* ADAM *and* PEGGY.

PHARAOH

Brad!

MABEL

Steve, don't worry! We'll find Adam, we'll bring him back!

JANE

He's headed for the Red Sea!

JANE *and* MABEL *run off, after* ADAM.

STEVE

I don't want him back! I want a new boyfriend! No, I want lots of new boyfriends! A new one every night, every minute! I'm sick of being in love! Where can I go? To meet every man who isn't Adam?

FTATATEETA

You want to go some place sensual, godless, and depraved?

STEVE

Tell me!

FTATATEETA

I'd say—Sodom.

STEVE

Sodom?

PHARAOH

(appalled)
Off-season? No . . .

STEVE

I don't care!

STEVE *stalks off, in the opposite direction from* ADAM.

PHARAOH

Let them go! Let them all go! I am the Boy-King of all Egypt! I am immortal!
(facing the audience, calling out to the hundreds of thousands of slaves)
Sing, gay slaves! Sing as you toil! Sing a gay slave song!

FTATATEETA

Sing to your Pharaoh!

GAY SLAVES

(recorded, a thousand voices strong, a song like "One" from A Chorus Line, *very bright and snappy)*

As the song continues, the PHARAOH *and* FTATATEETA *execute a crisp, choreographed vaudevillian strut and exit, in high show-biz style.* FTATATEETA *may have retrieved* PEGGY*'s spear and handed it to the* PHARAOH *earlier in the scene, and* FTATATEETA *and the* PHARAOH *might use their spears as props in their dance.*

Lights down on Egypt as the PHARAOH *and* FTATATEETA *dance off.*

STAGE MANAGER

A desperate prayer, go.

Lights up on MABEL*'s face; she stands downstage center, on a now bare stage. She is plaintive and yearning; she stands high on a mountain top, desperate and unsure of where to turn.*

MABEL

Dear God, it's Mabel. Of Canaan. Old Canaan.

(She glances down, collecting her thoughts; she looks up again, to heaven)

I know you've been doing your best. You've given life to—the world. But something's gone terribly wrong. There are tribes everywhere, at war with one another. There is disease, and pestilence, and—the media! People can't seem to live together, to appreciate what they've been given. And Adam and Steve—I don't know what to do! So I've decided that—it's up to you.

(with a new, tough-minded, gritty resolve, making sure God pays attention)

You made it, you fix it! It's time for . . .

(finding the word, for the first time in history)

a miracle!

STAGE MANAGER

Possible miracle, go.

The STAGE MANAGER *strikes a bell-tone on her chime.* MABEL *glances down, touching her stomach. She glances up, with a radiant smile.*

MABEL

(to God, very simply, overwhelmed)

Thank you.

JANE *enters, dressed as a shepherd, singing "Ave Maria." She brings* MABEL *a long blue veil and places it over* MABEL*'s hair.*

JANE

(singing)

AVE MARIA! GRATIA PLENA . . .

The stage is gradually transformed into a life-size Nativity scene. A manger, and perhaps fragments of arches or gothic windows, appear, designed in a glowing, painterly, Renaissance style. The entire cast appears, entering with a hint of procession, everyone joining in on "Ave Maria," possibly with a recorded backing, so the song soars and swells majestically. The actors should be dressed in robes and homespun, as shepherds, with head-coverings, sandals and rope belts. One shepherd leads a life-size, painted camel, another leads a life-size, painted goat. Another shepherd carries a painted sheep. The animals could be realistic, or have the flat, high-school charm of awkwardly painted props. Bales of hay appear. The shepherds and animals arrange themselves in a gorgeously traditional tableau, beneath a single, radiant star and a midnight-blue Bethlehem sky. The affect should be that of a Hallmark card, or a painted Nativity beneath a Christmas tree.

ENTIRE CAST

(singing)
MARIA, GRATIA PLENA
MARIA, GRATIA PLENA
AVE!
AVE, DOMINUS
DOMINUS TECUM . . .

ADAM *and* STEVE *have entered from opposite sides of the stage, costumed as Wise Men in flowing, glittering brocade robes and turbans. They each carry a gift in a small golden sack or box.*

STAGE MANAGER

Wiseguys, go.

ADAM *and* STEVE *leave the Nativity group, and approach each other downstage. "Ave Maria" gradually fades out.*

STEVE

Hey.

ADAM

Hey.

STEVE

Long time.

ADAM

How've you been?

STEVE

Sodom was *fantastic.* Of course, it was destroyed.

ADAM

By what?

STEVE

Tourists.

ADAM

Really.

STEVE

And you?

ADAM

Oh, you know. The burning bush, the promised land, the eleven commandments.

STEVE

Eleven?

ADAM

No white after Labor Day.

STEVE

Sure.

ADAM

Well, good to see you.

ADAM *starts to leave.*

STEVE

Hey—remember the flood?

ADAM

(turning)
Whoa. And Egypt?

STEVE

Right. And the garden?

ADAM

(passionately)
I missed you so much.

STEVE

I never got to Sodom.

ADAM

So will this be what you need? To finally believe?

STEVE

Mabel's baby?

ADAM

Mabel's miracle!

STEVE

We don't know that.

ADAM

I do! Because ever since Mabel got pregnant, I've been able to read my Bible!

STEVE

You have?

ADAM

(taking out his Bible and turning to various passages)

And I think it tells a story. So far, I can only make out a few words, but I think they're the most important ones. See?

(the first passage)

"Adam."

(another page)

"God."

(another page)

"Miracle."

(the title page)

"Copyright."

STEVE

Does it say "Steve"?

ADAM

Not yet. It's strange, so far it doesn't say anything about—us.

STEVE

But you want us to believe it. Every line. Without question.

ADAM

It's the word of God!

STEVE

But who wrote it down?

ADAM

(getting very angry)

Steve . . .

STEVE

(equally angry)

Adam . . .

ADAM

I don't want to fight!

STEVE

Same here!

ADAM

So—what did you bring?

STEVE

(holding up his golden sack)

Just—some frankincense. And you?

ADAM

(holding up his small brass box)

Myrrh.

STEVE

For a baby?

ADAM

(vehemently)

Babies love myrrh.

STEVE

How would you know?

ADAM

Well, nobody likes frankincense! Why don't you spend some money!

STEVE

I bet somebody just gave that to you and you're just passing it along!

STEVE *knocks* ADAM*'s gift out of his hands.* ADAM *knocks* STEVE*'s gift out of his hands.* STEVE *knocks* ADAM*'s Bible to the ground.* ADAM *smacks* STEVE *in the chest.* STEVE *hits him back. They begin to wrestle, falling to the ground and making loud grunting noises, a real schoolyard brawl.* STEVE *gets* ADAM *in a headlock.*

Say it!

ADAM

Say what?

STEVE

Say, "I love Steve more than anything," or I'll break your neck!

ADAM

Try it!

They wrestle again, just as viciously. ADAM *gets* STEVE *immobilized.*

Say it!

STEVE

What?

ADAM

Say, "I love myrrh!"

STEVE

Never!

They wrestle again, until ADAM *finally begs for mercy.*

ADAM

Stop it, stop it, time! Time!

They stop wrestling, lying in a heap on the ground, panting. ADAM *rises to his knees, and slaps* STEVE *on the butt.*

Steve!

STEVE

What?

ADAM

Will we still be like this, will we still be having this fight, in another thousand years? Another two thousand years?

We hear the continual beep of a cell phone. ADAM *and* STEVE *look around, puzzled as to the source of the sound.*

STEVE

Adam, that's you.

STAGE MANAGER

Two thousand years, go.

From within his robes, ADAM *removes a cell phone. He holds the phone out, unsure of what it is, as it continues to beep.* ADAM *stands.* STEVE *stands and rejoins the Nativity group.* ADAM *moves downstage, gradually figuring out how the phone works. He presses the button to speak.*

ADAM

(into his phone)

Hello? . . . I'm almost done, I'll be right home.

ADAM *stares at the phone with a mix of wonder and confusion. He presses the button to end the call. As he does so, we hear a bold, very rock and roll, Motown or pop arrangement of a Christmas song begin to blare over the PA system, something wildly propulsive and jubilant, an irresistible, wall-of-sound arrangement of "Jingle Bells" or "Sleighride", with a raucous, soulful vocal.*

As ADAM *listens to the music, he removes his wise man robe. Underneath, he is wearing very contemporary clothing, the modern-day outfit he will wear in Act II.*

ADAM *turns upstage to watch the Nativity. As the song soars, it begins to snow on the Nativity.*

STAGE MANAGER

Intermission, go.

ACT II

Time: *Chrismas Eve, the present.*

STAGE MANAGER

House to half, house out. Sound one eighty-five, go.

We hear the same sprightly Christmas song that ended Act I.

The curtain rises on Adam and Steve's modern-day loft in Manhattan. The loft is large and open but not too luxurious; while clearly designed, it still has a certain industrial rawness. There is a central, open archway, leading to a hallway, with the front door offstage. Additional doors or exits lead to a bathroom, a kitchen, and a bedroom.

The furnishings show more imagination than expense and include low shelves, a central couch, an armchair and ottoman, and several useful stools. A bar has been set out on a table or countertop, with plenty of liquor, soft drinks, ice, and glassware.

At the moment, the usual decor of the loft is completely obscured by an exuberant excess of Christmas glitz. There is a huge, fully decorated tree, surrounded by piles of gaudily wrapped packages. There are life-sized molded plastic Dickensian carolers, huge striped candy canes, an elaborate tabletop Nativity scene, an array of huge plastic Santas and snowmen, and plenty of plastic snowflakes and gingerbread people. The walls should be smothered in Christmas kitsch, including stockings, wreaths, and at least twelve reindeer pulling a sleigh, along with endless yards of evergreen garland and strand after strand of electric twinkle lights, as yet unlit. All of this has been carefully and lovingly thought out, by a true Yuletide freak, who believes that too much is just a starting point. There might be some Chanukah touches mixed in with the Christmas hurricane, including some Stars of David and a large plastic menorah atop the tree, where an angel usually roosts.

A Christmas Eve open house is being prepared. Colorful platters of food and treats have been set out, along with stacks of plates, utensils, and napkins.

In Act II, the STAGE MANAGER *can either stay seated at her desk beside the main playing area throughout the Act, or she can quietly exit after calling the first cues and return to call the end of the first scene, remaining onstage until her final exit.*

STEVE *enters from the offstage kitchen, carrying a punch bowl filled with eggnog. He wears basic, practical clothing, Levis and a sweater.* ADAM, STEVE, JANE, *and* MABEL *will be the same characters from Act I, only with no memory of that Act's events.*

STEVE *sets the punch bowl down on the bar. He turns off the Christmas music, which is emanating from either an audio system or one of those plastic Christmas trees with a singing mouth.*

We hear a key in the front door, and ADAM *enters, wearing a colorful scarf, a striped stocking cap, mittens and a winter coat. He is the ebullient Christmas fan, and he is bursting with holiday fervor.*

ADAM

Wait, just wait! One second!

STEVE

Adam . . .

ADAM

I saw it, we need it, you'll love it!

ADAM *runs back outside. He returns immediately, carrying a nearly life-size plastic reindeer with a bright red nose.*

STEVE

We don't have any more room!

ADAM

But we can't have a party without Rudolph! I was passing by Kmart, and it was the only one left, I had to wrestle it away from this woman with two screaming children, I said, I'm sorry, it's *mine*, you have deductions! Oh, and I also got . . .

ADAM *runs back outside.*

STEVE

No! You may not bring one more piece of holiday shit into this house!

ADAM *returns, carrying a large, molded plastic statue of the Virgin Mary.*

ADAM

But this is so special, this is actually sacred . . .

ADAM *places the statue on a table or counter.*

ADAM

It's the Virgin Mary.

STEVE

Yeah? So?

ADAM

Only—she speaks.

ADAM *pulls a cord, or presses a button at the base of the statue, and a perky recorded voice is heard, coming from inside the statue.*

VIRGIN MARY

Merry Christmas!

ADAM

It's a miracle. A modern miracle.

STEVE

Does she say anything else?

ADAM

I think she got the same tape as Barbie.

ADAM *presses the button again, and the statue speaks.*

VIRGIN MARY

Math is hard.

STEVE

I like that.

ADAM

(looking around, taking off his coat)

We have all the food and beverages and ice, and our Yuletide ambiance is almost complete . . .

STEVE

Almost?

ADAM

Shut your eyes.

STEVE

Are you gonna spray me with something?

ADAM

Shut them!

STEVE *shuts his eyes.* ADAM *turns off the regular lights, so the loft is in darkness.*

ADAM

One, two, three . . .

ADAM *flips a switch, or connects some extension cords, and all of the Christmas lights throughout the loft are illuminated. The effect is kitschy yet dazzling, real Christmas magic.*

ADAM

Open!

STEVE *opens his eyes; he is genuinely impressed with the lighting display.*

ADAM

Merry Christmas.

ADAM *and* STEVE *kiss; they remain deeply in love.*

ADAM

You look so great.

STEVE

(proudly, as in Act I)

I know.

ADAM

(gesturing to the room)

All of this—is for you.

STEVE

You are very sweet.

ADAM

I just want—to make every day of your life a Christmas party, from now on.

STEVE

Adam, I don't need parties . . .

ADAM

I do. Because I have something to celebrate—your life.

STEVE

Okay, how did it go?

ADAM

No, today isn't about me. No matter how phenomenal my day was.

STEVE

Tell me. I want to hear it. I mean it.

ADAM

(being noble)

No, I don't have to.

STEVE

Time's up!

ADAM

No! Okay! It was—incredible. It was, if I do say so myself, the most fantastic, deconstructed, trans-holiday pageant in the history of the elite Preston School first grade. Because I am not just a teacher, oh no. I am a post-modern, multi-cultural genius.

STEVE

"Trans-holiday pageant"?

ADAM

Well, I wanted to be inclusive because it's the right thing to do, and because the school is on the Upper West Side and the children's parents are all ultra-liberal, which means that when a kid hits somebody we say he's depressed. So I did the entire Nativity, the Wise Men, the shepherds, even the camels, only everyone in it—was gay.

STEVE

You're kidding.

The intercom buzzes.

ADAM

(as he moves toward the phone intercom hanging on the wall by the front door)

The kids *loved* it. The parents *loved* it.

(into the intercom receiver)

Hello? Right, three E, come on up.

(He buzzes the visitor in, and hangs up the receiver)

This one little boy, who played Jesus, he ran over to his mother, he was just beaming. And he said, "Mommy, I'm gay!" She was *thrilled*. She hugged him and turned to her husband and said, "Darling, this means *Yale!*"

STEVE

But—the Bible isn't gay.

ADAM

(triumphantly)

It is now!

STEVE

But—no. I think it sounds terrific.

ADAM

You do?

STEVE

Yes. And I am very proud of you. And so, at least for tonight, I am going to be—a Christmas person.

STEVE *takes the stocking cap off* ADAM'*s head and puts it on.*

ADAM

You?

STEVE

Yes. Because of everything you've done.

(as Santa)

Ho, ho, ho!

ADAM

(amused)

Stay back.

STEVE

Come over here, little boy, and sit on my lap.

ADAM

(sitting on STEVE*'s lap)*

Can I tell you what I want?

STEVE

I can tell you what you'll get.

ADAM

Santa!

(as ADAM *and* STEVE *embrace,* ADAM *pulls away)*

Steve?

STEVE

Yeah?

ADAM

Can I—no, I can't.

STEVE

What? What is it?

ADAM

It's just—there's something I need to ask you, and it's sort of major, beyond major, but—no, it's too weird!

STEVE

What? Ask me!

The doorbell buzzes.

ADAM

Later.

STEVE

Adam!

ADAM

It's fine.

(calling out, to whoever's at the door)

It's open!

CHERYL MINDLE *enters.* CHERYL *is a fresh-faced young woman, recently arrived from Utah; we met her early in Act I, in the audience. She wears a holly or Santa brooch on her winter coat and carries a potted poinsettia in foil. She is extremely perky and outgoing, and thrilled to be invited to* ADAM *and* STEVE*'s Christmas party. She is good-hearted and hugely enthusiastic about everything. She combines all the pep of a cheerleader, missionary, and fan club president. As she enters, she is dazzled and*

missionary, and fan club president. As she enters, she is dazzled and awestruck by the loft's Christmas decor.

CHERYL

Merry merry!

(looking around at the decor, she gasps)

Oh, *Adam!* Oh my God!

ADAM

Cheryl?

CHERYL

It's *gorgeous!*

ADAM

(thrilled)

Isn't it?

CHERYL

(sincerely, as a compliment)

It's . . . it's a *mall!*

ADAM

Steve, this is Cheryl Mindle, my new teaching assistant, from school. She just started.

CHERYL

And I love it! Adam, your pageant!

*(*CHERYL *removes her coat, revealing an extremely Christmasy outfit, including a sweater knitted with blazing red cardinals, a Santa or a Christmas tree, paired with a long, colorfully pleated wool skirt, red stockings, and clunky maryjanes. As* ADAM *takes her coat, she speaks to* STEVE*)*

You should have seen it, it was so touching!

ADAM

Cheryl's not going home for Christmas, so I asked her to come and help with the party.

CHERYL

(to STEVE*)*

And I have heard so much about *you!*

STEVE

Uh-oh.

CHERYL

And I love your loft! Now, you renovated this whole place yourself?

STEVE

I'm a contractor.

CHERYL

And you hate Christmas!

STEVE

Cheryl!

The intercom buzzes.

ADAM

No, it's going to be fine, Steve is being very festive.

STEVE

I am!

(trying very hard to be sincere, ferociously growling his good cheer at CHERYL*)*

Happy holidays!

CHERYL

That's good!

ADAM

Cheryl, this is the intercom, you just pick it up . . .

(speaking into the receiver)

Hi, come on up.

(to CHERYL*)*

And buzz.

(He buzzes the visitor in)

CHERYL

(impressed)

We don't have one of those, back in Misty Bluffs. That's where I'm from, in Utah.

STEVE

Are you—a Mormon?

CHERYL

Born and bred!

STEVE

(putting his arm around ADAM*)*

Are you aware that—we're gay?

CHERYL

(totally sympathetic and chipper)

Of course! And I am not judging you, uh-uh! Adam is a great guy, and I know that you've been together forever, I mean, way longer than most normal couples.

STEVE

Normal?

CHERYL

Uh-huh, and I know that some good Christians, like my Mom, think that gay people are sick and godless, but I said, no, Mom, they are sensitive and artistic!

(She gestures with both arms to all the Christmas decor as sincere proof of gay people's artistic glory)

STEVE

You go, girl!

CHERYL *whoops in agreement and gives a fervently physical, if awkward, two snaps up.*

CHERYL

Do you know what you need?

STEVE

Tell me.

CHERYL

Angels. They're real, and they're everywhere, watching over us. Back home, I have fifteen different hand-painted ceramic angels, three stuffed angels, an angel poster, an angel T-shirt, oh, and two pairs of angel pajamas!

STEVE

Cheryl, are you—seeing someone?

CHERYL

You mean, like a boyfriend?

STEVE

(after a beat)

No.

The doorbell buzzes, and ADAM *goes offstage, into the hall*

CHERYL

Stop it! I bet there are angels in this room, right now! I can feel it! Tonight is gonna be magical!

ADAM

(stepping in from the hall)

Ladies and gentlemen, a Christmas visitor!

TREY POMFRET *strides into the room. He is an acerbic, very gay man dressed as Santa Claus, including the padding, the red suit, the belt, the boots, hat, and a detachable white cotton beard and moustache. He carries a sack over his shoulder.*

CHERYL

(delighted)

It's Santa!

TREY

Fuck you!

CHERYL

(undaunted)

It's New York Santa!

TREY *rips off his hat, beard, and mustache, and heads straight for the bar, where he begins violently putting ice cubes into a glass and mixing himself a very stiff drink. He is furious, barely able to contain his rage as he tells his story.*

TREY

(to ADAM*)*

I am so pissed at you!

ADAM

At me? Why?

TREY

Because of all this Bible business!

CHERYL

Bible?

TREY

I am an over-bred, over-educated Wasp from Connecticut, so I've always thought of God as, you know—an ancestor. But lately Adam's been going on, about miracles, and his little Bible pageant, so I thought, well, I'll try.

(noticing CHERYL*'s poinsettia plant)*

Oh look, it's a poinsettia—the gift that won't die. So I don this ensemble and I volunteer, on Christmas Eve, at the local homeless shelter. Where I have just allowed countless heart-breakingly innocent, bright-eyed homeless children to sit on my lap. "Ho, ho, ho, and what would you like for Christmas, little Simbali, or Jamal, or Tylenol?"

(going over to shake CHERYL*'s hand)*

I can make these jokes because my name is Trey, and my brothers are named Shreve and Stone, so who am I to talk? And little Advil says, "Santa, whassup? Is you a faggot?"

CHERYL

No!

ADAM

What did you do?

TREY

Well, I took a deep breath, and I said, "Why yes I am, little Midol. And the North Pole is for everyone, gay and straight."

ADAM

That's perfect!

STEVE

And what happened?

TREY

Armageddon. The child's hard-working, down-on-her-luck single parent grabs the child off my lap and screams, "Get away, cocksucker!" To which I reply, "But darling, look what I've brought for you—Christmas crack." And finally the director of the shelter says that maybe it's best if *I* leave! So I come here, and my question for you, Adam, is this—what the fuck is God thinking?

ADAM

Trey, somewhere in that shelter was a gay kid, who got to see a gay Santa.

CHERYL

(going to fetch TREY *a drink)*

You need some eggnog.

TREY

(as he opens his jacket to remove the pillow padding; he wears a T-shirt under the jacket)

With a chaser.

STEVE

(to TREY*)*

This is Cheryl. She's from Utah.

TREY

Oh, I knew that.

CHERYL

How?

TREY

Your smile. Your glow. Your shoes.

CHERYL

Well, I think what you did was just tee-riffic!

ADAM

It's the true Christmas spirit.

STEVE

Oh no, oh no, I'm having a problem, staying Christmasy.

CHERYL

(flinging open her arms)

Hug alert! Woo-woo-woo!

CHERYL *runs across the room toward* STEVE, *to hug him.* ADAM *deflects* CHERYL, *as* STEVE *flees.* ADAM *goes to* STEVE.

ADAM

(to STEVE*)*

You can do it! For the baby Jesus!

STEVE

But Adam—you're Jewish!

CHERYL

You are? Really?

ADAM

(gesturing to all the Christmas decor)

Duh.

TREY

Of course.

The intercom buzzes.

CHERYL

No, let me!

(into the receiver)

Merry something! Come on up!

(She buzzes the visitor in and speaks to the room)

But you know, I always feel sorry for Jews. I mean, on Christmas Eve.

TREY

I know. When my sleigh lands on a Jewish rooftop, I always look down the chimney and yell, *"Nothing for Goldberg!"*

ADAM

But I want to be clear. I love Christmas, for the decor and the spirit, but I do not want to be Christian. Because my Aunt Sylvia told me, all gentiles are bitter alcoholics who drive German cars and beat their wives.

CHERYL

(immediately)

Adam! That is a terrible stereotype!

TREY

It's true, but it's a terrible stereotype.

MABEL *enters, bursting with giddy Christmas cheer. She wears a winter coat, a knitted Peruvian cap, huge knitted mittens, and mukluks. She carries a cardboard cake box.*

MABEL

Merry Christmas!

ADAM

Mabel!

JANE *enters. She wears an enormous, distended pair of overalls—she is hugely pregnant. Her belly juts out so far that she cannot close her down-filled coat. She is feverishly, gloriously livid. She has not been physically comfortable for months, and she can barely get around. Her volcanic fury, and her pregnancy, are at peak. Being pregnant has given her absolute authority to majestically blame the entire world for her condition. Her entire first scene is an aria of rage, directed at everyone in the room, at full bellow.*

JANE

There is no God!

STEVE

Jane.

JANE

(to ADAM*)*

I blame *you!*

ADAM

Me?

JANE

May you *burn!*

MABEL

(thrilled, to everyone)

Eight months and counting, raging hormones!

CHERYL

Eight months?

TREY

Jane, should you be here?

JANE

(to TREY*)*

Fuck you!

(regarding MABEL*)*

She tells me we should have a baby . . .

(regarding ADAM*)*

he tells me we should have a baby, everyone's telling me, a baby is a gift, why should gay people be denied!

ADAM

That's right!

JANE

Why? WHY? Because gay people used to be *smart!* But I listened, I said okay, we've been together for fucking ages, why not? A baby, a child, someone to send out for cigarettes!

MABEL

(to everyone, regarding JANE*)*

She quit, everything.

JANE

(regarding MABEL*)*

And she's looking up at me, with her shining little eyes . . .

(regarding ADAM*)*

and then he chimes in—"Come on, Jane! You're the lucky one!"

CHERYL

You're radiant!

JANE

(to CHERYL*)*

FUCK YOU! Whoever you are! I am not radiant! I am not a madonna! I am a WHALE! I am a WAREHOUSE! I've got this bloodsucker sitting in my stomach, and it's trying to punch its way out!

MABEL

It's a brand new life!

JANE

It's the *alien!* I am not supposed to be pregnant—I am a BULL DYKE! It's like if Ralph Kramden got pregnant! I can't stand it!

MABEL

(sincerely, doting on JANE*)*

Isn't she adorable?

JANE

Fuck childbirth! Fuck making a family! Fuck the miracle of life! Merry Christmas! I gotta pee!

JANE *exits, into the bathroom.*

TREY

This is so touching.

ADAM

It's a Hallmark moment.

MABEL

Isn't this *perfect?*

ADAM

Why?

MABEL

(chattering happily as she skips around the room, pulling many small, brightly wrapped gifts from the

shopping bags she and Jane have carried in. Some gifts will go under the tree, and others to party guests. As Mabel speaks, she will not feel sorry for herself, or get at all serious or solemn—she is on a complete Christmas and childbirth high.)

She's been like this for weeks. And at first I felt so helpless. I mean, I wanted this baby so badly, and I tried, I had all those treatments, I had that operation, but it just wasn't going to happen—oh, I love your tree, it's garish! So when Jane volunteered . . .

STEVE

Volunteered?

ADAM

Steve. . .

TREY

As a sublet. . .

MABEL

Yes! And I was so incredibly moved, I thought, oh my God, she would do that for me, for us? And all along, I've been wondering, what can I do to repay her, what gesture can I make that could possibly equal her incredible, selfless act? So I prayed.

STEVE

Good move!

CHERYL

That is so sweet!

(to MABEL*)*

I'm Cheryl. I work with Adam.

TREY

She's a Mormon.

MABEL

(thrilled)

Get out! I love Mormons!

CHERYL

You do?

MABEL

(sincerely)

They'll believe anything!

ADAM

So you prayed . . .

MABEL

Right, and I went to all different churches and temples and ashrams, and then finally I went to the gym.

TREY

The one true God.

MABEL

Amen! And I was doing this spinning class, you know, on the stationary bikes, and, as usual, I offer my fat up to God. And just as we're doing this amazing series of jumps, in and out of the saddle, and the instructor is playing all of these disco Christmas songs, I peak! I have an epiphany!

STEVE

You were dehydrated.

MABEL

And when I get home, I ask Jane—to marry me.

ADAM

Oh my God!

CHERYL

(whooping)

Whoa!

STEVE

Jesus.

MABEL

And she's sitting there, in her recliner, you know, sort of what she calls, beached? And she's watching her favorite show, *Xena*. And I stand in front of her and I say, "Jane, you are the co-mother of our child and the love of my life. Jane, my beloved, my giver-goddess, my exalted perfect other—will you marry me?"

ADAM

And she said . . .?

JANE *has emerged from the bathroom.*

JANE

"You're blocking Xena."

STEVE

Way to go!

As she and JANE *reenact the marriage proposal,* MABEL *will help Jane get settled into an armchair; sitting down, like everything else, is not easy for* JANE *in her current state.*

MABEL

And I grabbed the remote and I turned off the set and I said, "No! I know that I can't really share in the amazing and difficult upheaval you're experiencing—although I bet I can write a poem about it!"

JANE

She threatened me!

MABEL

"And I can make it better—you have to marry me!"

CHERYL

And she said . . .?

JANE

"Gimme the remote!"

ADAM

And you said . . .?

MABEL

"Not until you say yes!"

STEVE

That's blackmail!

JANE

And it was the episode where Xena was bathing Gabrielle!

MABEL

(triumphant)

So we're getting married!

JANE

I had no choice!

MABEL

And we were just wondering if, because you're our very closest friends, and you're all totally a part of us, if we could be married right here. Tonight.

ADAM

Tonight?

STEVE

Here?

MABEL

And we've invited this wonderful woman, Rabbi Sharon, to come to the party and perform the ceremony.

TREY

Rabbi Sharon? In the wheelchair? From cable?

MABEL

Yes! She has that show, it's so motivating, I watch it every morning, at six A.M.

ADAM

Of course—what's it called?

MABEL

Who Believes?

STEVE

Wait. You invited some handicapped, public-access lesbian rabbi to our Christmas Eve open house to marry you?

MABEL

I just dialed the number on the screen, "one-nine-hundred-Shebrew." I told her all about us, she was thrilled!

JANE

Please, you are in no way obligated. Even if the two of you did help get me into this fucking mess.

ADAM

Steve?

STEVE

Adam?

ADAM

I hate to say this, and Steve, you're gonna kill me, but—things are coming together. Steve is feeling so great, he's back at work, he's doing two lofts, I have just presented an all-gay Bible pageant, Jane is about to give birth, and now you're getting married—do you know what this sounds like?

TREY

All the reasons people hate New York?

ADAM

A celebration! We'd love to have the wedding here! We'd be honored!

STEVE

Why not? Merry Christmas!

ADAM *and* STEVE *kiss, as the intercom buzzes.* CHERYL *picks up the receiver.*

CHERYL

(into the receiver)

Hello, Rainbow Chapel! Come on up!

(she buzzes the guest in)

TREY

Will it be a Jewish ceremony? I'm sorry, I'm from Westport, but I did rent *Yentl.* Will there be that wonderful lighting?

CHERYL

Will there be those funny men, with the strange hair, all dressed in black?

TREY

Art dealers?

MABEL

And you know, Adam and Steve, if you want, Sharon could also marry the two of you.

ADAM

No, come on. We can't just decide to get married, on the spur of the moment, as part of a trend. Can we?

JANE

(needling them)

Can you?

STEVE

Adam, I love you, you know that, I hope everyone knows that, but—why do gay people need to get married?

MABEL

Because we're entitled!

STEVE

But have you noticed how conventional gay people are getting?

TREY

And wholesome?

JANE

We registered.

CHERYL

For a lesbian wedding? Where?

JANE

L.L. Bean.

MABEL

And I have made a savory vegan wedding cake. We could share it.

CHERYL

Vegan?

MABEL *has opened the lid of the cake box, to admire the wedding cake.* TREY *and* CHERYL *peer into the box.*

MABEL

It means that it contains absolutely no animal products. Nothing suffers.

TREY

Except the people who'll eat it.

MABEL

No! It's delicious, it's tofu, and the frosting is made from soy powder and kelp.

TREY

What are the bride and groom?

MABEL

They're two hand-carved wooden seagulls. Because scientists have discovered that there are a great many lesbian seagulls.

CHERYL

How can they tell?

TREY

The ponchos.

JANE

(feeling a physical tremor)

Whoa!

MABEL

(running over to JANE*)*

Sweetie?

JANE

No, I'm fine, I think.

MABEL

(rubbing JANE*'s back)*

Find your core, like they told us at the birthing center . . .

CHERYL

The birthing center?

JANE

We're in this class, with ten other pregnant lesbians. It's like *The X-Files*. This one woman, she wants to give birth underwater, to reduce trauma to the baby. I said, what are you having, a *trout?*

KEVIN MARKHAM *enters.* KEVIN *is a hot young go-go boy. He wears a long overcoat, boots and a red elf hat. He is a giddy, muscled Chelsea specimen, with just a hint of Valley Boy syntax.*

KEVIN

Like, Merry Christmas! I can only stay a few minutes, I'm working a party down at Twilo.

MABEL

On Christmas Eve?

KEVIN

I'm a go-go elf.

KEVIN *flings off his coat, revealing just a g-string, or a red wrestling singlet, either garment should have a cluster of mistletoe attached at the crotch.*

TREY

Mrs. Claus and I are so proud of him.

KEVIN

How's my baby?

KEVIN *runs to* JANE *and kneels, putting his head on her stomach.*

JANE

Stop that! I hate it when people do that! I'm not ticking!

KEVIN

But it's so great!

CHERYL

Wait—

(regarding KEVIN*)*

is he the baby's father?

KEVIN

(proudly)

I'm the godfather.

CHERYL

So—who's the Dad?

ADAM

(shyly, but bursting with pride)

Me.

CHERYL

You?

ADAM

I'm the donor.

CHERYL *screams and runs to hug* ADAM; MABEL *deftly intercepts the hug, and* ADAM *joins* STEVE *on the couch.*

CHERYL

Congratulations!

ADAM

But it's really only technical . . .

(to JANE *and* MABEL, *being respectful)*

we signed a contract, I have no legal rights to this child.

MABEL

(to ADAM *and* STEVE*)*

But you know that we want you, both of you, to be part of the baby's life. And we are so grateful for your sperm.

TREY

I always say that the next morning, over coffee.

MABEL

We need all of you. It takes a village to raise a child.

TREY

Greenwich Village.

JANE

Everyone is pitching in. You promised!

CHERYL

(starting to circulate, offering guests a bowl of chips or pretzels)

Do you know yet? If it's going to be a boy, or a lesbian?

MABEL

We all went together. We had an ultrasound.

ADAM

You could see her, she was so tiny.

JANE

(fondly)

She was smoking.

CHERYL

What about a name?

MABEL

Well, we've been thinking about something biblical . . .

CHERYL

I love that!

ADAM

Like Sarah . . .

KEVIN

Or Rebecca . . .

JANE

Oh, or my favorite . . .

CHERYL

(offering JANE *the bowl)*

What?

JANE

Satan.

CHERYL *stares at* JANE, *very taken aback. After a beat, she sharply pulls the bowl of snacks away from* JANE, *and moves across the room, as far from* JANE *as possible, glancing back at Jane with horror.*

CHERYL

But who makes the ultimate decisions? Like, what religion will the baby be?

STEVE

That's interesting. We haven't really talked about that.

MABEL

I'd like to expose the baby to all possible faiths, and let her make any final decision . . .

ADAM

But we can read her Bible stories.

STEVE

Why?

ADAM

Because they're wonderful stories!

JANE

About, oh, guilt and punishment . . .

CHERYL

But what about angels, huh? They're always totally good, and they watch over us, and guide us . . .

TREY

Darling, please. Angels are just Prozac for poor people.

MABEL

Trey!

ADAM

I know. We can take the baby to the Easter Show at Radio City. It's the perfect introduction to the life of Christ.

TREY

Jesus and the Rockettes. I always wish they'd do the Last Supper. "Which of you shall betray me?"

(He looks around, selecting an imaginary showgirl-Judas, and pointing to her)

"Could it be—Lisa?"

STEVE

So Adam, religion is just about glitz.

ADAM

But why not? Isn't that the best part? There's even that one Broadway theater, the Mark Hellinger, that they've rented out as a Baptist church. It makes a strange kind of sense.

TREY

Because it's where gay men once gathered, to worship Carol Channing.

ADAM

Yes! And I've been changing the Bible. I've been making the stories more gay-positive, and upbeat.

STEVE

Then why bother having a Bible at all?

ADAM

So the baby can know, about God.

STEVE

Not in my house.

ADAM

Your house?

KEVIN

Wait, you guys, everybody! Maybe I can help!

ADAM

Please!

KEVIN

Last night, when I was dancing, I had—a vision.

MABEL

A vision?

KEVIN

Okay, this is gonna sound really weird, but—you know what it's like, when the music is fantastic, and the whole crowd is really hot and really into it, and you're on, like, some incredible acid?

A beat, and then everyone in the room looks at everyone else and nods, "Sure, of course."

KEVIN

(now standing on an ottoman)

And I was up there, on my box, wearing like, my boots and, what was it, oh yeah, a washcloth, and the light hit me! And I looked right into it, and—there she was. Like floating, gazing down at me.

MABEL

The Virgin Mary?

KEVIN

(with awe)

Olivia Newton-John. Who I always loved from when I was, like, little, and I watched her in *Grease,* where she was like this sort of Australian exchange student, and then in this other flick, *Xanadu,* where she was this goddess who comes to earth and teaches this, oh, this really cute guy how to do roller disco!

TREY

It's her Lear.

KEVIN

And she always seemed like, well, maybe not a great actress, but like a really nice lady, and then I read where she had cancer, but she's doing good, and I'm telling you, she was up there, and she spoke, she said . . .

TREY

"Have you never been mellow?"

MABEL

(to TREY*)*

Hush!

KEVIN

She said, "Congratulations! You're going to be part of a baby." And that's the first time it really hit me, like a whole new deal—a baby! I mean, all of us, are we qualified? To have a kid? And I said, Livvy—that's what her friends call her—Livvy, is this right? Is this what God wants?

MABEL

(eagerly)

And what did she say?

KEVIN

She said—that maybe the baby is going to be *really special.*

JANE

Like what? Like who?

MABEL

You mean, the baby could be what Adam's been talking about, about everything coming together . . .

ADAM

Maybe!

The intercom buzzes.

CHERYL

(on her way to the intercom)

You mean, Jane's baby could be—the Messiah! The Second Coming! Right here in Chelsea!

KEVIN

It could happen!

TREY

We already have three Starbucks!

STEVE

No, come on, guys! Don't do that to a baby!

JANE

Don't do that to me!

During the previous conversation, CHERYL *has privately buzzed the next visitor in.*

ADAM

But what if the baby is part of the answer. To my question. The question that's been ruling my life.

STEVE

Which is?

ADAM

Well, it's just that I'm afraid to ask it, out loud . . .

STEVE

Try!

JANE

(feeling a very sharp labor pain)

Awww!

MABEL

Honey? Should we—should I call an ambulance?

JANE

No! I'm just, oh God—I am so embarrassed!

MABEL

Why, sweetie?

JANE

I mean, you guys know me, don't you? I strip paint. I haul cinder blocks. I'm Jane, right?

MABEL

Of course, honey.

JANE

But it's just, I've been getting so—emotional. Just yesterday I was rebuilding a carburetor, and—I burst into tears.

TREY

(sympathetically)

You too?

The doorbell buzzes.

CHERYL

I'll get it.

CHERYL *runs out into the hall.*

JANE

And I've been getting—so scared. I'm turning into such a wuss. I'm not a wuss, am I?

EVERYONE

(very touched)

Awww . . .

JANE

Shut up!

CHERYL *wheels in* RABBI SHARON, *in her wheelchair.* SHARON *is an aggressively confident, gung-ho woman, a cable TV diva with a mission. She is stylishly dressed and coiffed, and immediately takes center stage. She relishes an audience, and a challenge; she's a star.*

SHARON

Shalom!

MABEL

Sharon!

SHARON

(to the room)

That's right—I'm a disabled lesbian rabbi. Gimme your money!

MABEL

Sharon!

ADAM

(going to SHARON, *offering his hand)*

Hello. Welcome. I'm Adam.

SHARON

(shaking his hand)

Yes you are!

ADAM

And this is Steve.

SHARON

(to STEVE*, totally upbeat)*
The guy with AIDS, am I right?

STEVE

You got it. Mabel?

MABEL

And this is Jane.

SHARON

(very excited)
Who's pregnant!

JANE

No, no. It's beer.

SHARON

So, does everyone watch my show?

MABEL

Only every day!

KEVIN

I tape it! It is so inspirational! Like that time in April, when you wore your hair up?

SHARON

The Power Look for Passover!

MABEL

I loved that!

SHARON

So let's hear it! I'm Rabbi Sharon, and welcome to . . .

EVERYONE

(copying SHARON*'s signature arm gesture, in which she points in a wide, sweeping half-circle, and then points to heaven)*
"Who Believes"!

SHARON

All right, let's get goin'! I've got two basic weddings—with God and without.

KEVIN

What's the difference?

SHARON

Well, with God is non-sectarian but focused on a higher power, with a pronoun of your choice. God can be He, She, It, Our Mother, Our Father, Our Sister Spirit, Our Lavender Light, The Goddess, The Creator, The King, or Our Lord.

TREY

Excuse me—are those the specials?

JANE

And without?

SHARON

(eyeballing TREY, *sizing him up)*

Uh-huh!

(to everyone)

Without is more inner, it's the union of souls, the joining of two perfect beings, let our community bless this day, you get the picture, we hate God—but we want gifts! So?

MABEL

Well, I'd really like to have God, but not if it's going to make anyone uncomfortable.

SHARON

(to the room)

Kids? Everyone? God? Hands?

There is a beat, as everyone looks at each other, slightly unsure. Then, as everyone raises their hands except for TREY *and* STEVE

ADAM: Sure!
CHERYL: Of course!
KEVIN: Go for it!
JANE: Why not!
(all at once)

SHARON

Great! That takes care of the mindless sheep. Santa?

TREY

I'll pass.

SHARON

Mister Kringle?

MABEL

Trey?

TREY

I'm sorry, I'm having a problem, with the entire Judeo-Christian everything.

SHARON

Tell me.

TREY

Well, most of your major-league atrocities are committed in the name of someone's god. And can you tell me any big-time religion that isn't especially vicious to, say, women and gay people?

JANE

Just one.

TREY

Which?

JANE

Oprah.

MABEL

But that's all just interpretation. God doesn't hate anyone.

TREY

I do!

MABEL

Trey . . .

TREY

Oh, all right. Do you know the only thing I really like about God?

SHARON

Spill.

TREY

The art. It's my favorite thing in the world. There's a small private chapel, in the Medici Palace in Florence. And the walls are covered with frescoes, by Tintoretto, it's the *Adoration of the Magi*, but the colors are so delicate, and there's so much gold, that it looks like—Cinderella. I have never seen anything so beautiful.

SHARON

Bravo. And the wedding?

TREY

Fine. God. Maybe.

CHERYL

Sharon? I believe. And I'm a Mormon!

SHARON

(after a beat)

No, come on, really.

CHERYL

I am! And I think that God is just the best thing ever!

SHARON

Baby, your religion is like—ten minutes old. It was founded by some guy who got caught, cheating on his wife. She said, so where were you, and he said, well, um, um, I met this . . . angel, and she gave me . . . the Book of Mormon! If he'd told the truth, you'd be worshiping a waitress.

CHERYL

Why is everybody picking on Mormons?

TREY

This is New York, dear. You're the Jew.

STEVE

But why are we? Have you ever seen or listened to, a Chasid or a Buddhist monk or the Pope? The only thing that separates their magic tricks from Scientology is a few thousand years. That's the blink of an eye.

CHERYL

Right! So why pick on anyone?

STEVE

No, Cheryl. Pick on *everyone.*

SHARON

And Steve. So handsome.

STEVE

Is that a bribe?

SHARON

Nope. You I respect.

STEVE

Why?

SHARON

Because I've heard you're stubborn. You say show me. You say no.

STEVE

You heard right.

SHARON

Because God did you wrong. AIDS. The homeless. The Holocaust.

TREY

The subway.

STEVE

So?

SHARON

I still believe.

TREY

Why?

SHARON

Because otherwise—I have nothing.

STEVE

You have common sense. You have reality.

SHARON

And self-pity.

STEVE

Excuse me?

SHARON

Come off it. You think about God more than anyone else in this room. Why you? Why now?

STEVE

No, I don't!

SHARON

(physically pursuing STEVE, *in her wheelchair, really going after him, picking a fight)*

And why not? God made you sick! And not your neighbor, not some fascist dictator, not some creep.

STEVE

It's a virus!

SHARON

Come clean, baby! It's God!

STEVE

Fuck you! And fuck God!

SHARON

Now we're talkin'! Siddown!

STEVE *hesitates; he doesn't sit.*

SHARON

(gesturing to her wheelchair)

I am.

STEVE, *grudgingly, sits.* SHARON *moves her wheelchair into a position to face the group.*

SHARON

Five years ago, it's Sunday morning, and I'm walking down Christopher Street, on my legs. And I've just done a bat mitzvah, for my gorgeous niece, and I'm carrying my latte, my heavenly date-nut scone, and the Sunday *Times*, and I'm headed back to see my naked young girlfriend. And then—a bicycle messenger. Outta nowhere, he swipes me, my legs go out, the *Times* goes flying, and I'm slammed smack—into the back of a FedEx truck. Which doesn't see me, so, as I'm lying in the street with a broken hip and five fractured ribs, it backs up onto my pelvis. FedEx truck tires! And then—it goes forward, right in my ribcage—crack! And by this point, people are screaming and pointing and then, and I swear, I am not making this up, I am a person of God—a rusty air conditioner falls off a twenty-story building, onto my face! And, as I finally lose consciousness, thank you, I see that bicycle messenger *eating my scone!*

And I come to, three weeks later, paralyzed, half-blind, and I think, what the fuck is going on? Not just why me, but why the fucking air conditioner? And some nurse gives me this book, called *When Bad Things Happen to Good People*. And all I'm thinking is, I don't care! What I want to know is, why do *good* things happen to *bad* people! I'm in a wheelchair, and Saddam Hussein's in a Mercedes. I can't walk, and O.J.'s on the ninth hole. I'm paralyzed, and Brooke Shields has a series!

And then—it hits me. What doesn't? Why it happened. And what I'm supposed to do, with my useless legs and my messed-up life and my deluxe new nose—do you like it?

(She gestures to her nose)

"The Mindy." So I buy me some airtime and I say, listen up, New York! Take a look!

(She gestures to herself and her wheelchair)

This is your nightmare! This is the ice on the sidewalk, the maniac in the hallway, this is God when she's drunk! So if I can still believe, if I can still thank someone or something for each new day, if I can pee into a bag and still praise heaven for the pleasure, then so the fuck can all of you, mazel tov, praise Allah and amen!

KEVIN

I love her!

SHARON

And you know something? Sometimes God delivers. Like these new drugs, these cocktails, am I right?

MABEL

You see?

SHARON

(*to* STEVE)

Are you on them?

STEVE

You know it. Twenty-eight pills a day.

SHARON

Twenty-eight prayers. Twenty-eight mitzvahs.

MABEL

Twenty-eight miracles.

STEVE

That is science. And luck.

ADAM

That's God! Steve, do you remember our Christmas party last year?

STEVE

We didn't have one.

TREY

Oh, thank God, I thought I wasn't invited.

ADAM

Mabel had just given birth. To a baby, a boy who lived for two days. In the same hospital where you'd spent the last two weeks, at 125 pounds, hooked up to a torture chamber, coughing up blood. And I sat in that waiting room, and I cursed God. I said, no more desperate prayers, you get down here, you fix this, or—fuck you forever. And tonight—look at Jane. Look at you.

SHARON

Look at all of you.

(*regarding* CHERYL)

Even the Martian.

CHERYL

Mormon!

ADAM

All right, Sharon, you're a person of God, right?

SHARON

With a Web site and a T-shirt!

ADAM

What does it say?

SHARON

"Oy Gay."

ADAM

So maybe I can ask you—my question. The one I've been trying to get brave enough and strong enough to ask.

SHARON

I can't wait!

ADAM

No, I shouldn't bother you with it, I'll just shut up . . .

EVERYONE

ADAM!

ADAM

All right! Here goes. All year long, maybe all my life, things have been—building. To this morning. When I woke up and I looked at Steve, who was curled up, snoring, and—smiling. And I looked out the window and it was snowing, just gently, just that perfect MGM snow. And I got my coffee, and I realized that, at exactly that second—I was . . . happy.

SHARON

Mazel tov!

ADAM

No! I ducked, I shivered, I was terrified! I thought, no, don't jinx it, don't call down a flood or a thunderbolt! And ever since then, I've been in this blind panic. So—is it okay? To say it, to feel it? To be in love, to be part of a baby, to have a party, to be—happy?

SHARON

You're Jewish, right?

ADAM

You noticed.

SHARON

(with genuine compassion, very straightforward)

Sweetheart, I talk to God, all the time. And you know something? God says yes.

ADAM

Yes?

SHARON

Yes.

ADAM

Okay. All right. Since you say so. I am going . . . to be . . . happy.

ADAM *looks around the room, at everyone, ending on* STEVE. *He shuts his eyes, facing out. A beat. He tilts his head upward. He mouths the words "Thank you." He smiles.*

SHARON

(after a beat, to STEVE*)*

So—how about another miracle? Right now?

STEVE

What?

SHARON

A wedding. With God? You're the holdout.

ADAM

Steve?

STEVE

(after a beat)

Fine.

SHARON

Damn, I'm good! Mabel? Wedding party?

JANE

Adam and Steve—you're the best men.

ADAM

Our pleasure.

ADAM *and* STEVE *line up near* JANE *and* MABEL.

CHERYL

(picking up the poinsettia, for use as a bouquet)

What about a Maid of Honor, huh?

TREY *and* KEVIN *both raise their hands. Realizing they are in competition, they face off.*

TREY

This is a sacred occasion, and we are both politically ideal gay men.

KEVIN

So there's, like, only one way to settle this.

TREY

Slap fight.

TREY *and* KEVIN *start to slap each other viciously, yelping like fiendish, depraved schoolgirls.*

MABEL

You guys! You can both be our People of Honor!

KEVIN

(gesturing, for TREY *to take a place with the wedding party)*

Father Christmas.

TREY

(gesturing for KEVIN *to take a place)*

Employee.

TREY *and* KEVIN *stand with* ADAM *and* STEVE *and* JANE *and* MABEL, *who are gathered in a group near* SHARON. CHERYL *is about to join the group, when a thought strikes her:*

CHERYL

Uh-oh, um, wait—you all seem like wonderful people, but if I participate in a gay wedding, if I don't leave right now, will I go to hell?

TREY

(rapidly)

Would you rather have a roomful of homosexuals talk about you after you've gone?

The entire wedding party leans toward CHERYL, *a bit menacingly.*

CHERYL

I'm in!

CHERYL *joins the group, or pulls up a stool nearby.*

SHARON

(taking out her Bible)

Tonight our community gathers—female and male, lesbian, gay and bisexual—yeah, right. And is anyone here transgendered?

TREY

Cheryl?

CHERYL

What?

SHARON

(to CHERYL*)*

Good for you!

(CHERYL *looks very confused)*

And now, a lesbian wedding, or as I like to call it, their second date. With the blessing of Our Lord, by Rabbi Sharon. All right. Jane?

JANE

Right here.

SHARON

Do you love Mabel?

JANE

(gazing into MABEL's *eyes)*

Yes.

SHARON

And Mabel?

MABEL

Before the eyes of God?

SHARON

Sing it, baby!

MABEL

Yes. No.

JANE

Mabel?

MABEL

(with great difficulty)

Not always. When my baby, when our baby, died—I hated everyone.

JANE

I know . . .

MABEL

And when you tried to give me everything that had been taken away—I hated you.

JANE

Oh, babe . . .

MABEL

So I bought a gun.

SHARON

(raising her arm and forming a gun with her forefinger; she makes a clicking noise, as if cocking the trigger)

A piece!

MABEL

A three fifty-seven Magnum. I wanted to do something that was—the opposite of me. And I went to this shooting range, in a warehouse out in Queens, and down at the far end of the alley, where they have the target, I had them put up pictures of Jesus, and Buddha, and Calista Flockhart!

ADAM

Calista Flockhart?

ALL THE WOMEN

Please.

MABEL

And then I had them add—a picture of Jane.

JANE

Oh my God . . .

MABEL

A Polaroid, from the day we found out you were pregnant. And I put on my protective plastic goggles, and I raised my Magnum, I held it straight out, and—I fired.

(holding out her arms, as if firing a pistol, really going through it)

I blasted 'em, one after the other, Jesus, BLAM! Buddha, BLAM! Calista—*eat something!* And Jane—I hesitated, I thought, I can't do this, I can't kill you, but then I thought about my baby, and your belly, and that fucking home pregnancy stick with its little pink plus sign, and—*blam!*

JANE

And—how did you feel?

MABEL

Fantastic. It was this incredible rush, I realized, they're not dead, none of them, but I had killed—my rage, and my envy. And I ran down to the target and I took down your picture and I looked at your face, well, at your chin, and—I kissed it. Because I love you *so much.*

JANE

Oh my God.

SHARON

Jane?

JANE

My water broke!

This revelation sends the room into a frenzy of activity, as ADAM *and* MABEL *tend to* JANE, *while everyone else tries to figure out a course of action.*

KEVIN

Her water?

SHARON

Where's the doctor?

MABEL

I'll beep her!

SHARON

Call an ambulance!

JANE

Right now!

CHERYL

Oh my God!

TREY

What should we do?

SHARON

What do you need?

STEVE

(on the phone)
Hello? I need an ambulance!

JANE

St. Vincent's!

STEVE

(into phone)
For St. Vincent's. From two nineteen West Ninteenth Street. Three E. It's an emergency!

CHERYL

(who has run into the bedroom and returned with JANE*'s coat)*
Tell them it's the Messiah! They'll come faster!

TREY

(to CHERYL*)*
You're so young.

MABEL

(at JANE*'s side)*
Start the breathing, focus on me . . .

ADAM

Should we get her downstairs?

JANE

I'm fine, I'm fine, I can get there . . .

ADAM *and* MABEL *start walking* JANE *toward the front door.* JANE *collapses; everything is happening very fast.*

JANE

No I can't!

SHARON

No she can't!

MABEL

Oh my God!

STEVE

How about the couch?

ADAM *and* MABEL *start walking* JANE *toward the couch.*

JANE

The couch is good . . . oh my God . . . NO, NO!

KEVIN

She doesn't like the couch!

TREY

Can you blame her?

ADAM

What about the bedroom?

MABEL

Sweetie?

JANE

Fine! Whatever! AWWW!

*(*MABEL *and* ADAM *get Jane into the bedroom, as Jane moans and screams. Exiting.)*

GODDAMNIT!

JANE, MABEL, *and* ADAM *are offstage.*

STEVE

(having hung up the phone)

The ambulance is coming, but they said it's Christmas Eve, so it might take some time . . .

CHERYL

I think we should all go in there, and gather around the bed and hold hands, in a birthing circle!

KEVIN

All of us?

CHERYL

We can help the baby be born into a world of hope and trust!

SHARON

It's worth a shot!

STEVE

Let's go!

Everyone runs into the bedroom; STEVE *pushes* SHARON*'s wheelchair. The stage is now empty; a beat. Then we hear the guys emit a truly bloodcurdling group scream, from the bedroom.*

ADAM, STEVE, TREY, AND KEVIN

(from offstage)

AWWWW!

ADAM, STEVE, KEVIN, *and* TREY *all hurtle out of the bedroom, gasping with terror; they scatter, clinging to various pieces of furniture.* ADAM *pours himself a stiff drink.*

TREY

Oh my Lord . . .

KEVIN

I mean, I know that's how it works, but . . .

ADAM

I am *so* gay!

From the bedroom, we hear CHERYL *emit an even more bloodcurdling scream.*

CHERYL

(from offstage)

AWWW!

ADAM

Cheryl?

CHERYL *runs out of the bedroom, ricocheting across the room, even more grossed out than the guys.*

CHERYL

I am never having a baby!

SHARON *appears, at the bedroom door.*

SHARON

Nice work, all of you! She's in labor, big time! Any word on the ambulance?

ADAM

Not yet.

STEVE

(already on the phone)

I'm calling the hospital, maybe someone can talk us through it.

SHARON

Good man! I can use another pair of hands!

CHERYL

I can't!

KEVIN

I'm a dancer! I need my hands!

STEVE

(to the group)

I'm talking to a doctor, and I think he's gay . . .

(into the phone)

Yes, hello, it's an emergency . . . what?

(flirtatiously)

Jeans and a sweater . . .

ADAM

Steve!

SHARON

There's a woman giving birth!

JANE

(from the bedroom)

FUCK YOU!

SHARON

Trey!

TREY

Oh, all right, I'll pretend I'm a glamorous nurse, on a soap opera!

SHARON

Move it!

TREY

(on his way toward the bedroom)

I'll need hair spray!

STEVE

(on the phone)

Trey, he says to keep her on her back, on the bed, with one hand behind each knee . . .

TREY

(flirtatiously)

Not now, Doctor!

TREY *pushes* SHARON*'s wheelchair, and they both exit into the bedroom.*

STEVE

(on the phone)

He says there's going to be a lot of blood, so think about the sheets.

ADAM

What's on there?

STEVE

The Calvin Kleins. The periwinkle.

ADAM

(panicking)

The new ones?

KEVIN

I love those!

ADAM

JANE!

ADAM *runs to the bedroom door;* TREY *meets him, carrying the Calvin Klein sheets in a bundle, which he hands to* ADAM.

TREY

We stripped the bed.

ADAM

Thank you!

TREY

You should see this, it's sort of extraordinary. But I just can't picture my mother doing it.

ADAM

Maybe she was unconscious.

TREY

No—it was before six.

JANE *howls offstage, and* TREY *runs back into the bedroom.*

STEVE

(on the phone)

He says she shouldn't try to push, or she could tear!

ADAM

(yelling into the partially open bedroom door)

She shouldn't try to push or she could tear!

STEVE

(on the phone)

He says, keep your hand on her perineum!

ADAM

(into the bedroom)

Keep your hand on her—

(turning to STEVE*)*

her what?

STEVE

(on the phone)

The area between her vagina and her rectum!

ADAM

(struggling for a beat; he can't bring himself to say it, and then, into the bedroom)

Don't push!

TREY *runs in from the bedroom.*

TREY

It's happening. It's sort of quasi-neo-semi-miraculous. This creature is demanding to be born. This incredibly messy—Tintoretto.

STAGE MANAGER

Lights two fifty-four, go.

Blackout.

STAGE MANAGER

Lights two fifty-five and the miracle of birth, go.

From the darkness, a pin spot comes up center-stage on JANE*'s face and upper body. She is a mess, drenched with sweat, in the process of giving birth. She is standing, and we see her bare arms and shoulders. She has a dark sheet wrapped around the rest of her body. She might have the sheet wrapped at her waist, with her breasts exposed; the nudity should be totally the choice of the actress playing* JANE.

JANE

FUCK SHIT PISS! FUCK SHIT PISS COCKSUCKER CUNT! Get it out of me! I'm glad they have white carpeting!

(She starts the rhythmic breathing)

Right, right, don't push, let the baby come out by itself, good baby, natural baby, sweet baby, FUCK YOU DICK-LICKING BITCH CUNT! GET OUT OF MY BODY!

(She resumes the breathing)

Look at Mabel, focus on Mabel, she's covered with sweat, and blood, my blood, her mouth is open, it's like she's watching the sun come up in the Garden of Eden, FUCK MABEL! I WANT A HOSPITAL, I WANT DRUGS! Oh my God, here it comes, the baby's head—CHOP OFF ITS HEAD! WHY DO BABIES NEED HEADS! This just proves one thing, God is a buttfucking, motherfucking MAN! YOU'RE KILLING ME . . .

Oh my God, it's out! It's out of me, it's gone, oh my God, this is like the best orgasm I ever had! I love not being pregnant! Just let me lie here, forever . . . wait. Mabel's holding the baby, it's breathing, dear God, let it be healthy, and God, let it go to boarding school. Jesus fucking Christ, I'm a mother! Don't tell anyone! I have a baby . . . she's all ugly and wrinkled. She looks *mean.*

(finally accepting the baby, reaching out her arms)

Come to Mama.

The STAGE MANAGER *strikes a crisp, bright note on the chime.*

STAGE MANAGER

Lights two fifty-six, go.

The lights fade on JANE, *to black.*

STAGE MANAGER

Lights two fifty-seven and post-partum, go.

Lights up on the loft. It is a few hours later. Only ADAM *and* STEVE *remain, cleaning up after the party.* STEVE *carries a small plastic waste-basket. They are both still stunned by the evening's events.*

ADAM

We're fathers.

STEVE

Sort of.

ADAM

We've been fathers for almost two . . .
(He checks his watch)
no, three hours.

STEVE

How do you feel?

ADAM

Well, Trey was amazing, but I thought that Kevin was going to faint, when Mabel handed him the placenta.

STEVE

And a fork.

ADAM

And was it my imagination, or once we got to the hospital, was Rabbi Sharon hitting on Cheryl?

STEVE

Really?

ADAM

They were sitting very close, and I heard Rabbi Sharon whisper, "Once you've had a disabled lesbian rabbi, you never go back."

STEVE

It's true!

ADAM

Steve?

STEVE

Yeah?

ADAM

They've—stopped working, haven't they?

STEVE

What?

ADAM

The pills. The new ones. After Jane gave birth, I ran into the bathroom, to see what we had for pain. And I noticed, all of your bottles—they're empty.

STEVE

(after a beat)

Yup.

ADAM

Were you—were you going to tell me?

STEVE

Look, they don't work for everyone, and no one's been on them that long, and the side effects are worse than the disease, the whole thing was a crapshoot, I mean, come on.

ADAM

Steve?

STEVE

What?

ADAM

How long have you known?

STEVE

I don't know, a week, what difference does it make?

ADAM

It makes a difference.

STEVE

Why?

ADAM

Because I can't believe I said all that bullshit at the party! And you let me!

STEVE

I let you?

ADAM

I said I was happy! I said it was possible! I said that the heavens were smiling down on everyone, while you just sat there!

STEVE

What should I have done? Stood up and said, sorry folks, party's over! Especially for me!

STEVE *angrily takes the wastebasket out into the hall.*

ADAM

(starting to follow him)

Yes! Because that's the truth! And I can handle that!

STEVE

(re-entering)

You? And the truth?

ADAM

Why not?

STEVE

Adam—you have spent your entire life lunging for answers and miracles and your little kiddie pageant! You have devoted yourself to everything but the truth!

ADAM

But you're the one who's been lying!

STEVE

Fine! You want some facts? Hard-core?

(very simply, straightforward, without histrionics)

I'm dying. And this could very well be our last Christmas together.

ADAM

(going to him)

Steve . . .

STEVE

(backing away)

No! Fuck you! *Handle it!*

ADAM

(after a beat)

Okay. You're right. You're absolutely right. No more—questions. You are going to die. And I am going to watch you. You win.

ADAM *sits in the armchair. A long beat of silence. Then* STEVE *goes to the Christmas tree and selects a wrapped gift. He brings the gift to* ADAM *and offers it.*

ADAM

Not now.

STEVE

Please?

ADAM, *still resisting, takes the gift, and removes the wrapping paper. He then meticulously smooths and folds the wrapping paper, to save it. Then, overtaken by anger, he smashes the wrapping paper into a ball and throws it on the floor.* ADAM *opens the box. Inside is a beautiful sweater.*

ADAM

Oh my God. You got it. This is just what I wanted. This is cashmere. This is Armani. This cost a fortune.

STEVE

So—do you feel better now? About my dying? And losing your faith?

ADAM *looks at* STEVE. *He looks down at the sweater. He is overwhelmed by the insanity of the whole situation. He strokes the sweater, almost laughing.*

ADAM

Yes.

STEVE

(smiling)

There you go.

Adam puts the sweater aside and stands up. He faces out, gesturing to God.

ADAM

(to God)

Fuck you forever.

STEVE

Who are you talking to?

ADAM

I have no idea.

STEVE

Exactly. Believe in that.

ADAM

In nothing?

STEVE

In not knowing. In never knowing.

ADAM

How?

STEVE

Stop looking for comfort, or reasons, or peace. I don't need that. I never have. Take a real risk. Ask nothing. Know nothing.

ADAM

(after a beat, trying to see things Steve's way, and then)

I can't!

STEVE

Why not?

ADAM

I need . . . a story.

STEVE

A story?

ADAM

I can't believe in the Virgin Mary, not anymore. But I can believe—in Jane, and Mabel. And I can't believe in the baby Jesus. But I can believe in our baby, little Satan. And I won't tell her about the Garden of Eden. But I will tell her—about Central Park.

STEVE

Central Park?

ADAM

And the day we met.

STEVE

May third. Ages ago.

ADAM

Lunch time. The first really fabulous day. And I took off my shirt, to feel the sun.

STAGE MANAGER

Central Park, go.

Scenic elements from the Garden of Eden return, along with the garden's idyllic lighting. If possible, the loft might vanish or recede. As the garden returns, ADAM *and* STEVE *pull off their shirts, basking in the sunlight.*

ADAM

And I thought, I love this park. And I love this city. And I love the air and the breeze and the lake. And I'm alone. And then I turned.

STEVE

(smiling)

Hey.

ADAM

Hey.

The sultry, sexy saxophone music from the garden is heard. ADAM *and* STEVE *walk toward each other. As they are about to embrace:*

STAGE MANAGER

Curtain, go.

The curtain begins to descend.

ADAM

Wait! Hold on! Hold everything!

The curtain freezes.

ADAM

(to STEVE*)*

I'm sorry! One second!

(to the STAGE MANAGER*)*

You! That voice! The Stage Manager. Are you God?

STAGE MANAGER

(after a beat)

Well, I think I am.

ADAM

(with overwhelming yearning)

But are you really God? I still need to know! Have you really made everything happen? You have to tell me!

STAGE MANAGER

No I don't. I don't have to tell you anything. What do you want from me? I've been doing my job, and now I'm into overtime . . .

(She checks her watch)

No! I'm done! That's it! I'm outta here!

The STAGE MANAGER *pulls off her headset, grabs her script, and strides off the stage and out through the audience.*

STAGE MANAGER

(on her way out)

You people!

The STAGE MANAGER *leaves the theater, by a rear or side exit.* ADAM *and* STEVE *watch her go, amazed. After a beat we hear from outside the theater: TAXI!*

ADAM *and* STEVE *look around. Then they look at each other, mystified but elated—something has been released. Whatever happens next is up to them.*

ADAM

What's next?

STEVE

It's your call.

ADAM

(after a beat)

Sound one ninety-two, go.

An instrumental, bluesy version of "Have Yourself a Merry Little Christmas" is heard; it's very romantic.

STEVE

Merry Christmas.

ADAM *goes to* STEVE, *and they embrace and begin to kiss.* STEVE *makes* ADAM *aware that an audience is watching them.*

STEVE

Adam?

ADAM *sees the audience. He wants some privacy. With a mixture of sexual anticipation and great good humor, he says:*

ADAM

Curtain, go!

Mr. Charles, Currently of Palm Beach

For Peter Bartlett

Introduction

I wrote *Mr. Charles, Currently of Palm Beach* out of love and spite. It was written for the blissful Peter Bartlett, who played the title role when the play was first staged, at the Ensemble Studio Theater, in 1998. This production was perfectly directed by Christopher Ashley, and featured Ross Gibby as Shane, Mr. Charles' ward. Watching Peter and Ross rehearse and perform this play was, for me, a form of theatrical rapture.

As to the play's content, I will let Mr. Charles speak for himself. Try and stop him.

—PAUL RUDNICK

MR. CHARLES, CURRENTLY OF PALM BEACH premiered at the Ensemble Studio Theater in New York City on May 11, 1998, directed by Christopher Ashley, with the following cast:

MR. CHARLES .... Peter Bartlett
SHANE .... Ross Gibby
RECEPTIONIST .... Kate King
BABY .... Cameron King

Time: *Early evening.*

Place: *A bare-bones, public-access television studio in Florida. A video camera is mounted on a tripod and aimed at a platform that supports the flamboyant, if limited set for* MR. CHARLES' *cable show. There is a suitably fussy folding screen, a small, ornate French writing desk, holding a silver tea service and a floral arrangement, and a gilded, throne-like French chair set center stage. There is a small table beside the chair.*

Buoyant, big-band theme music is heard, something very upbeat and welcoming.

MR. CHARLES *enters. He is ageless. He is stylish, haughty, and bold. He wears a fairly obvious, fairly blond hairpiece, a tomato-red blazer over a linen shirt, with an Hermès scarf knotted apache-style at his throat, colorful espadrilles, white, lemon, or lime-green slacks, and a necktie knotted as a belt. His face boasts a not particularly discreet coat of moisturizer, bronzer, and a touch of mascara. His image is not transvestite, but Palm Beach decorator or antiques dealer. He is glorious.*

After smiling and posing for the audience, MR. CHARLES *sits on the throne-like chair. He picks up a letter from the small table.*

MR. CHARLES

(reading from the letter)

"What causes homosexuality?"

(He puts down the letter)

I do. I am so deeply homosexual, that with just a glance, I can actually turn someone gay.

(He glances at someone in the audience)

Well, that was easy. Sometimes, for a lark, I like to stroll through maternity wards, to upset new parents. I am Mr. Charles, and I am currently residing here in Palm Beach, in semi-retirement. In exile. You see, I was asked to leave New York. There was a vote.

Today's modern homosexuals find me an embarrassment. This is because, on certain occasions, I take what I call—a nelly break. For example: a few months ago, I attended an NYU conference, on gay role models. And this young man stood up and said,

(in an earnest, manly voice)

"We must show the world that gay people are not just a pack of screaming queens, with eye makeup, effeminate hand gestures, and high-pitched voices." And I just said . . .

(He does a nelly break, shrieking and flapping his wrists)

It just happened. I went nelly.

Oh, or another time, I was attending a rally. And a woman approached me, and she said, "I would like you to donate five thousand dollars, to support our boycott of Hollywood films which portray homosexuals as socially irresponsible, promiscuous, and campy."

(another nelly break)

And so, I was asked to leave the city. As revenge, I have begun to broadcast this program on cable channel forty-seven, a show which I call "Too Gay." It can be found at four A.M. on alternate Thursdays, in between *Adult Interludes* and *Stretching with Sylvia*. Poor dear.

I would now like to welcome my delicious studio audience. Hello, everyone!

(He gestures to the audience)

And let's also introduce another popular feature of this program, my devoted companion, Shane.

SHANE, *a dim, affable, low-rent young hunk enters, wearing a tight tank top, warm-up pants, and sneakers.* SHANE *eyes the audience and the camera.* SHANE *and* MR. CHARLES *get along just great; they appreciate each other.*

SHANE

(to the audience)

Hey.

MR. CHARLES

Shane is my ward. I first met him three weeks ago, at a fabulous local nightspot, the Back Alley. Shane was appearing atop a plywood cube. He is a gifted performer. Shane?

SHANE *nods and moves downstage so he is standing directly in front of the camera, head down.* MR. CHARLES *motions to a sound booth, and hot dance music blares.* SHANE*'s head jerks up, and he begins to dance, first in his version of slow seduction, which quickly explodes into a demented frenzy.* MR. CHARLES *then motions for the music to stop, and* SHANE *stops dancing.*

MR. CHARLES

Thank you, Shane.

SHANE

You got it.

SHANE *exits.*

MR. CHARLES

Since I have begun these broadcasts, I have received many letters and postcards, including this telegram, from the National Gay Task Force in Washington.

(He picks up a telegram from the table)

It reads . . .

(reading the telegram)

"Dear Mr. Charles. Stop."

(He puts down the telegram)

I would now like to answer several of the many queries I have received, regarding homosexuality. Shane?

SHANE *enters, now wearing a homemade Robin costume, which includes tight green trunks, a yellow satin cape worn over a tight red tank top, and a black mask. He is not happy about this outfit. He carries a stack of letters, which he dumps on the table. Then he poses, with his hands on his hips, as a superhero.*

SHANE

Man, I don't know about this outfit.

MR. CHARLES

It doesn't bother Robin.

SHANE

I ain't Robin.

MR. CHARLES

Oh, but you could be.

SHANE

I mean, what is the deal with Robin anyway?

MR. CHARLES

He's adorable.

SHANE

Yeah? Do you think that Batman and Robin, like, do it?

MR. CHARLES

Do you?

SHANE

Yeah. I bet that like, after they nail some robbers and save Gotham City, they're, like, all fired up, so they, like, do some

K and stay out all night and then they pick up like, Spiderman —he's hot—and the Incredible Hulk, and they all go back to the Batcave and jump in the, like, Bat-jacuzzi, and then Superman flies in and some of the Power Rangers, like the blue one, and the X-Men, and then they all have an orgy and then they see the Bat signal in the sky, only Batman says, fuck, I can't fight no more crime, I'm too wasted. And then they all crack up, and, like, pass out, wouldn't that be cool?

MR. CHARLES

Indeed. And we could dress up and go in their place. Only we would fight—bad taste. We would burst into people's homes and proclaim, "We have come to save you! From that terrible armoire!"

SHANE

Okay.

SHANE *exits.*

MR. CHARLES

He hides his pain.

(He picks up a letter)

"Dear Mr. Charles, Is there really a cure for AIDS?" Well, I've heard about these new treatments—some of my friends are swallowing fifty-eight pills, every day. It's a tribute—to Judy. I swear, only a gay disease could be treated with something called a cocktail. Why not a parfait?

(He picks up another letter)

"Dear Mr. Charles, Should gays be allowed to serve in the military?" Oh, no. Congress is absolutely right. You see, I have this military fantasy. Shane?

SHANE *enters, now wearing fatigue shorts, an olive-green military tank top, and a military cap.* SHANE *places the video camera on his shoulder and follows* MR. CHARLES *during the next segment, acting as* MR. CHARLES' *personal cameraman.*

MR. CHARLES

I'm serving in Vietnam, with my unit. And one night, I traipse into the shower tent. It's after hours, and I'm just wearing my kimono, mules, and a light moisture pack. And I hear the sound of rushing water . . .

*(*SHANE *discreetly makes the sound of rushing water)*

and I turn, and there at the end of a row of showers stands a naked marine—Colin Powell. His flesh glistens as he lathers up, he runs the soap over his firm chest, his already generous belly, down, down into his manly areas. My breathing grows heavy as my kimono falls from at least one shoulder, and I stand beneath the showerhead beside Colin, attaching my plastic shower caddy, which contains my shampoo, conditioner, finishing rinse, and scented bath geleé. My eyes are everywhere, feasting on his shining, sudsy, gleaming male flesh. Finally, I speak. "Hello, soldier," I murmur. "Don't you just hate those Vietcong?" No, darlings, we have no place in the armed forces. Make remarks, not war. Thank you, Shane.

SHANE *reattaches the camera to the tripod and exits.*

MR. CHARLES

(picking up another letter)

"Should gays be allowed to marry?" Of course, wealthy older women.

(another letter)

"Can you always tell if someone is gay?" Well, I can. There's always a giveaway, sometimes it's just a glance on a street corner, or a slight moan during oral sex.

(another letter)

"Dear Mr. Charles, I am a lesbian."

Doesn't that sound like some marvelous first line from Dickens?

"I am a lesbian. All you do on your show is talk about gay men. What about gay women?"

(He stands and smiles, very graciously)

Lesbians. I could write a cookbook. But let us not resort to easy stereotypes, picturing all gay women as husky, can-do gals out hiking in their flannel and sensible shoes. A gay woman is not simply Paul Bunyan with a cat.

(By this point MR. CHARLES *has poured himself a cup of tea from the silver tea service. He notices that* SHANE *has neglected to provide a lemon wedge on the tray. He calls out, sharply)*

Shane?

SHANE *hurries in, holding out the lemon wedge, which he squeezes into* MR. CHARLES' *cup of tea.*

MR. CHARLES

Danke, Shane.

SHANE *exits.*

MR. CHARLES

Lesbians are charming, endlessly varied people, with all sorts of haircuts, from the flattop to the pixie. I, in fact, have taken a lesbian into my home. She's asleep in the basement, until Spring.

(another letter)

"How can I raise gay—positive children in today's political climate?"

Well, there are many politically aware children's books, including *Daddy's Roommate* and *Heather Has Two Mommies*. I will soon be publishing my additions to this series: My children's books will include *Uncle Patrick Has a Beautiful Apartment* and *Aunt Cathy's Large Friend.*

(another letter)

Oh look, here's a letter for Shane.

(He sniffs the letter, which is perfumed)

Oh, Shane!

SHANE *enters.*

SHANE

Yeah?

MR. CHARLES

(pointing to the words as he reads)

"Dear Shane."

*(*SHANE *grins and grunts, very pleased)*

"I think that you are the hottest thing in south Florida. I loved you on last week's show, when you were dressed as Tarzan."

(The Tarzan outfit was MR. CHARLES' *idea, and* SHANE *grimaces at the memory.* MR. CHARLES *is triumphant.)*

You see? "But why don't you dump Mr. Charles and get your own show?"

SHANE

(pleased)

It says that?

MR. CHARLES

Well, Shane, do you think you're ready?

SHANE

Well, you know, I've been thinkin' about it. Like, I could come out and like dance, and then . . .

(a big thought)

talk about stuff.

MR. CHARLES

(encouragingly)

That's good.

SHANE

And then I could, like, put up my beeper number and, like, do this look.

MR. CHARLES

Which look?

SHANE *turns away for a second, and then turns back to the camera, delivering his version of a sultry, orgasmic look.*

SHANE

And I'd go, I'm Shane, and I'm into full body massage, hot oil wrestling, and I'm an abusive top.

MR. CHARLES

(thrilled)
I can see it!

SHANE

Oh, and ya know what I wanna call it? My show?

MR. CHARLES

Yes?

SHANE

(a huge thought)
"The Shane Show."

MR. CHARLES

By all means!

SHANE

(into the camera)
Watch for it!

As SHANE *exits, he pauses when standing right in front of the camera, and executes a demented martial arts/karate move, with a cry of "Hyah!" He exits.*

MR. CHARLES

They grow up so fast.
(another letter)
"Dear Mr. Charles, Do you enjoy gay theater?" I am gay theater. All right, I will now give you the entire history of American gay theater, in sixty seconds. Go!

MR. CHARLES *stands, and there is a dramatic lighting change, as he free-associates rapidly.*

MR. CHARLES

"Jimmy isn't like the other boys—*do you know what you are*—he's no son of mine! I'm just so lonely and sick of my own evil—he was a boy, just a boy—Bill was my buddy, and our love was pure and strong, but those things they're saying—they're true, about me! I'm so sick and ashamed, Karen! *Do you know what you are?* I am a thirty-two-year-old, pockmarked Jew fairy, and that was when my father saw me backstage; in my wig and my tights, and he said, take care of my son.

(singing)

I am what I am!

(in a gravelly voice, as Harvey Fierstein)

I just wanna be loved, is that so wrong? But Doctor, what's wrong with David, with all the Davids? Our people are dying, and the Mayor still won't even say the name of the disease—Maria Callas!

(He raises his arms as graceful wings)

Let the great work begin!

(He raises his arms again)

Let the great work begin, part two! When you speak of gay theater, and you will—be kind. Because it's all about love, valour, and gratuitous frontal male nudity!

SHANE *enters, naked, and hands* MR. CHARLES *a bouquet of roses.*

MR. CHARLES

Bravo!

SHANE *exits.*

MR. CHARLES

We have now come to my favorite part of the program, a forum which I call, "People I *Hate*." This week's person I hate most in the world is someone I've never even met. His name is Theodore DiBenedetto, and he wrote this letter to the editor of our local paper.

MR. CHARLES *reads aloud from a copy of the newspaper, using a butch voice.*

MR. CHARLES

(reading from the paper)

"Dear Palm Beach Sentinel, I am a gay man who owns the East Bay Hardware Store."

(He looks up, with a withering glance, and then continues)

"And I am sick and tired of gay people demanding equal rights when they keep behaving like freaks. As gay people, we must prove that we aren't just stereotypes. We must demonstrate that our lives are normal and wholesome. We must show that we can hold jobs, go to church, and raise children, just like anyone else. That is how we will earn our place at the table."

(MR. CHARLES *puts down the paper. He is now dangerously angry, like steel.*)

Darling, I *set* the table. I arranged the flowers. And I would rather have Shane's knife at my throat than share even a brunch with Mr. DiBenedetto and his kind. The nice boys. The good citizens. But please, Mr. DiBenedetto, if you'd like, by all means, be normal and wholesome and responsible. Get married, have children, move to the suburbs. I'll wait here. Oh, and Mr. DiBenedetto, by the way . . .

MR. CHARLES *stands and launches a viciously savage nelly break, directly into the camera. He becomes a ferocious nelly whirlwind, making enormous, flamboyant gestures to the audience. He might look into the camera and elaborately mime applying lipstick and slicking each eyebrow. Finally, he turns, rump to the camera, and minces back to his chair, his heels off the ground, as if he were wearing imaginary spike heels. He turns, sits, and arranges his wrists. With a knife-edge flourish, he crosses his legs.*

SHANE *enters, wearing white jeans and an unbuttoned Versace shirt.*

SHANE

Um, I gotta go out, okay?

MR. CHARLES

Do you have to get your hair cut?

SHANE

Yeah, um, right!

MR. CHARLES

Did you take the car keys?

SHANE

(holding up the keys)

Right here!

MR. CHARLES

(like a doting parent)

And all of the cash on my dresser, my credit cards, and my mother's emerald earrings from my sock drawer?

SHANE

Got 'em!

MR. CHARLES

Do you love me forever?

SHANE

Yeah, of course!

MR. CHARLES

(delighted)

On your way!

SHANE

Later!

SHANE *exits.*

MR. CHARLES

He's not fooling me. He doesn't need a haircut. Ah, but I am the last of my kind. I shall perish, like the dinosaur. Unless of course, Steven Spielberg discovers some ancient DNA from Paul Lynde and makes more.

(He picks up a final letter)

"Dear Mr. Charles, Have you ever been in love?" Oh, yes. I fell in love quite early, I must have been, oh, twelve? I had just been savagely beaten, by . . .

(He tries to remember, quite cheerfully)

oh, it could've been anyone. But this was at school. I came home bruised, caked with mud. I ran up to my room, and I looked in the mirror. And I thought, all right, whom would I rather be? The boys who beat me up, the boys who played baseball and caught frogs and were already losing their figures? Or would I rather be—Mr. Charles. Who even at twelve knew how to turn his face so the tears would glisten. Who knew enough to immediately put Billie Holiday on the hi-fi, and lip-synch. Who could transform a schoolyard humiliation—into an Academy Award. And that was when I fell passionately in love—with being gay, Oh, there have been men, and boys, and Wedgewood. But being gay—there's a romance.

SHANE *enters.*

SHANE

Um, Chuck?

MR. CHARLES

You're back.

SHANE

When I was drivin' to the club, I was thinkin' about, like, what you said at the beginning of the show, that you can, like, make people gay, just by lookin' at 'em?

MR. CHARLES

In my time.

SHANE

Well, I was kinda wonderin', I mean, a lotta gay guys have kicked, right? Which is like, for me, you know, bad for business. I mean, it's not like Florida's empty or nothin', but what I was thinkin' is, could you make some more? To fill the place up?

MR. CHARLES

Oh no, I don't think so, nobody wants to be truly gay anymore. It's passé.

SHANE

So, like, kick their ass! You could do it. Like, make more of you. Use your superpowers. Your gay ray. Make an army. A planet!

MR. CHARLES

It's tempting . . .

SHANE

Go for it, man!

MR. CHARLES

You're too sweet.

SHANE

Later!

SHANE *exits.*

MR. CHARLES

Well, let me see, how would I do this? Make more?

(He looks at the audience)

Yes—the receptionist. With the baby. Could you come up here?

The studio RECEPTIONIST *comes up onstage, carrying her 7-month-old baby. The receptionist is sweet and apologetic.*

RECEPTIONIST

I'm sorry, my babysitter cancelled, and I had to bring the baby to work.

MR. CHARLES

How lucky! What a beautiful child. Boy or girl?

RECEPTIONIST

A boy. Max.

MR. CHARLES

(to the baby)

How would you like to grow up—like me? How would you like to be—Mr. Max?

RECEPTIONIST

Can you really make him—like you?

MR. CHARLES

Is there a problem?

RECEPTIONIST

Well—will he have a difficult life?

MR. CHARLES

Who doesn't?

RECEPTIONIST

Will people be mean to him, just because he's gay?

MR. CHARLES

(cheerfully)

Of course.

RECEPTIONIST

Will he do those—nelly breaks?

MR. CHARLES

Sometimes—in front of your parents. Think how upset they'll be.

RECEPTIONIST

(firmly, holding out the baby)

Do it.

MR. CHARLES

If you insist.

MR. CHARLES *aims two fingers at the baby and makes a small hissing noise, zapping the baby.*

MR. CHARLES

There you go!

RECEPTIONIST

Thank you.

(as she exits, to the baby)

He's a very nice man.

MR. CHARLES

(to the mother and child)

Have fun! He will!

The RECEPTIONIST *and baby exit.*

MR. CHARLES

(to the audience)

Anyone else? Oh, I know what you're thinking. You're thinking, oh please, he doesn't really have any powers. He's just another shrill, aging Palm Beach queen with too many cocktails and a bad hairpiece. Well, would you like to hear something even more horrible, my pretties? It isn't a hairpiece.

MR. CHARLES *cackles gleefully and gestures grandly to his hair, mouthing the words, "It's mine." The peppy theme music from his show is heard, and he makes a little pouting face; then he begins blowing kisses and waving goodbye, as the lights fade.*

The following is an alternate, abbreviated ending for this piece. It has been used on occasions when no live baby was available—using a doll or a bundle seemed impossibly wimpy. The changes for this version begin just as Shane makes his final exit.

MR. CHARLES

Oh no, I don't think so, nobody wants to be truly gay anymore. It's passé.

SHANE

So like, kick their asses! You could do it. Like, make more of you. Use your superpowers. Your gay ray. Make an army. A planet!

MR. CHARLES

It's tempting . . .

SHANE

Go for it, man!

MR. CHARLES

You're too sweet.

SHANE

Later!

SHANE *exits.*

MR. CHARLES

Well, let me see, how would I do this? Make more? Well, I am on television. Someone's watching. There are all those people out there, waiting for Sylvia.

(into the camera)

Hello, everyone! In your pajamas and leotards! Hello, Florida! Guess what?

(He points his fingers at the camera and makes a hissing noise, zapping the viewing audience)

Oh, I know what you're thinking. You're thinking, oh please, he doesn't really have any powers. He's just another shrill, aging Palm Beach queen with too many cocktails and a bad hairpiece. Well, would you like to hear something even more horrible, my pretties? It isn't a hairpiece.

MR. CHARLES *cackles gleefully and gestures grandly to his hair, mouthing the words, "It's mine!" The peppy theme music from his show is heard, and he makes a little pouting face; then he begins blowing kisses and waving goodbye, as the lights fade.*